SONS OF GODS

-First Testament-

WRITTEN BY

DAVID KULCSÁR

True wisdom comes to each of us when we realize how little we understand about life, ourselves, and the world around us.

-Socrates-

†

No man or woman born, coward or brave, can shun his destiny.

-Iliad-
Book VI

†

Thou art mine hammer, and weapons of war: for with thee will I break the nations, and with thee will I destroy kingdoms, and by thee will I break horse and horseman, and by thee will I break the chariot and him that rideth therein. By thee also will I break man and woman, and by thee will I break old and young, and by thee will I break the young man and the maid.

-Holy Bible (1599, Geneva)-
Jeremiah 51:20-22

A NOTE FROM THE AUTHOR

Whether one believes in a God or not, it is without question that one of the greatest gifts mankind was given is the power of imagination. Every culture of every part of the world has made use of it, and indeed, is a rare facet of shared humanity.

I have always been fascinated by Greek mythology and its heroes. Equally, I have also had a great interest in the Bible and its similarities with the legends of the Greeks. Both are also equally violent and filled with war; God alone is directly responsible for millions of deaths in the Old Testament by the time the reading is done.

I always had a burning curiosity as to why the Western world, after thousands of years of polytheistic worship, went so suddenly to a monotheistic view of the world. No faith, no story, no mythological legend had ever explained this chasm.

So, using that special human talent of imagination, I set out to create my own mythical tale; one that I hope you, the reader, finds to be an entertaining journey of love, loss, war, and self reflection. I certainly found entertainment in writing it.

--David Kulcsàr

CHAPTERS

-A-PROLOGOS-A-

Muses, sing!
Sing, immortal voices, of this world's time,
Blemished with the blood
of both Gods and Mortals.
Sing of the land where Heroes great did stride,
Sow the seeds of history far and wide.

Sing of the ancient Beasts who once so roamed,
Sing of the fire that rained like Heaven's tears,
Sing of the False One with conquest's hunger,
Who in his wake left the Gods asunder.

Sing of Him who was the last son of Gods,
Sing of the Seven who held firm their faith,
Sing of Him who so claimed His rightful throne,
Whose legacy the songs of Man intone.

Sing of Him whose strike let Baal's last breath slip
into the soft breeze of fate and her song,
Sing of Him who let loose the storms of war,
Whose grief and spite swept like a tidal bore.

Sing of the land where Heroes great did stride,
Sow the seeds of His legend far and wide.

-I-GENESIS-I-

~There were giants in the earth in those days~
Genesis 6:4

Every world across the vast expanse of the Universe has a Spirit Mother.

They came to be when the cosmos itself was born, destined to act as caretakers and overseers of their worlds. Three such worlds, Mars, Venus, and Earth, orbited one of the countless millions of suns in the Universe. Gaia, the Spirit Mother of the Earth, Enyo, the Spirit Mother of Mars, and Eileithyia, the Spirit Mother of Venus, gave unto their worlds the air, the water, and the trees.

On Earth, Gaia created the great Lizard Beasts who roamed the lush jungles and forests of the world. For thousands of years and countless generations, these giant creatures did live their lives under her careful watch. To help rule the world, Gaia created the Twelve Titans, naming Kronos as their King.

On Mars, Enyo created a creature she called Man, and within several centuries, their cities dotted the many rivers and valleys of Mars. Man became masters of war, the land, and law.

On Venus, Eileithyia created a creature called Woman, and they became masters of logic, love, and the home.

Jewels,
Green and shining in a dark, cosmic sea,
Three worlds of endless, reaching Gardens
whose beauty deceives the shrouding darkness,
Living alone in a false tranquility.

They were all ignorant of a dark power lurking in the far reaches of the cosmos. On a world made of ice, covered in endless, lifeless tundra, ruled a powerful God. This God, not satisfied with his own world and tinged with a hunger for conquest, proclaimed himself to be the one, true God of the Universe.

Over the course of countless millennia, he travelled world to world, bent on destroying every God and every civilization that did not proclaim allegiance to him. They all resisted, but none succeeded, and in his wake, worlds were left barren and lifeless.

It was only a matter of time before this evil was to discover the lush worlds of Earth, Venus, and Mars. Gaia, while sitting in her Garden of Life, saw Enyo and Eileithyia come down from the sky. Weary and battered, they carried with their powers the last remnants of their people, setting down into the

Garden two of Man and two of Woman. Gaia raced over, and the Spirit Mothers of Venus and Mars, in their dying breaths, bemoaned that a great evil had vanquished their worlds and reduced them to cinders. They entrusted Gaia with the last of their creations and died.

It was then that a great ball of flame roared down from the sky with the might of a thousand thunderclaps.

The Heavens so bled of red hot fire,
Flaming down the tears of a weeping sky,
The Earth turned into a burning pyre,
The embers licking the stars far above.

Upon its impact, the Earth shook mightily and a sea of flame did set ablaze the jungles and unsuspecting Lizard Beasts. Gaia used her powers to preserve the Garden of Life, but was left horrified at the sight of her world. Ash and smoke poisoned the sky, blotting out the sun, withering all life that did breathe of it.

The Titans watched from atop Olympus in an awe of fury as their kingdom was reduced to ash. As quickly as the world had been engulfed in flames and life destroyed, the Heavens began to weep of snow and much of the lifeless Earth was glazed in ice.

The crater, far below and still smoldering, cut deep into the crust of the world, spanning a great distance in length and depth.

Like a specter,
Rising from a hollowed grave deep below,
The silhouette of a man glistening
in an armor of blackened bronze and gold,
Coming forth from the smoke like boats in fog.

Hair as black as midnight's highest hour,
Skin colored dull ash like cindered, dead coals.
Eyes a hollow blue in their icy stare,
Glowing with conquest's ravaging hunger.

Kronos, in a voice that boomed, called down from Olympus.

"Who dares decimate my Kingdom?!" he bellowed. "To set foot upon my Earth, and destroy the life that I rule?"

The dark God, glaring up at the summit of Olympus, shouted his answer in a tone of ferocious calm.

"I am great, O Lord Kronos, for there is none as weak as you, and there is no truer God than I. I am Baal, and I have come to claim this world."

Kronos and the Titans, humored by this bold sentiment, laughed heartily. Zeus, the eldest son of Kronos, stepped forward, offering to rid them of this vagrant God. Kronos did chortle and grin at this proposal, naming instead his own brother, the Titan Krios, to the task.

Krios, with his spear and shield, gladly accepted the duty, and leapt from the summit of Olympus whilst the other Titans and their brethren watched in great anticipation.

Roaring,
With a mighty cry did brave Krios charge,
Who tossed his spear with all his might,
Tip piercing swiftly through the bitter air
as it glistened under Heaven's soft light.

The spear so struck upon mighty Baal,
Yet the shaft cracked and the spear tip shattered,
A sharp rain of broken bronze and splinters
fell into the snow.

The Titans above gasped, struck by an astounding fear they had never known. Baal held out his hand, and in that instant, the clouds above did split. There came crashing down, like thunder from the sky, a spear of blackened bronze into Baal's hands.

Krios quickly lifted his shield and drew his blade, planting firm into the icy soil.

Krios raised his sword and sturdy shield,
Charging forth with a Godly might so brave,
Yet his shield split in half and sword cracked,
His eyes filled heavy with mortal dismay.

The Titan stumbled into the snow, scampering like a frightened animal. It was then that Baal followed Krios with a sinister elegance, placed a foot upon his neck, and snapped it in half like a sun baked twig. A ghostly silence carried on through the windswept ice and snow. Baal glared up at the summit of Olympus, his voice carrying across the empty, desolate world.

"Your world is mine. You are mine. If you do not wish to bow down to your True Lord, then you are not the first nor last whom I will destroy. I have swept away everything on countless worlds. I have reduced the wicked to heaps of rubble. I will crush you and destroy every last trace of your world so that even the memory of you will disappear."

Kronos, enraged, gave a roar that shook the skies, and he leapt from the summit of Olympus with his spear. The other Titans followed, whilst Zeus and his young siblings watched the battle from above. The Titans came crashing down, their spears and arrows burning through the frozen air. Baal, however, was far too fast and powerful, and the Titans were struck down, one by one.

How the mighty and great so quick do fall
to the spear of Baal,
A fluid elegance in war and death
that drew the Titan's final breath.

Kronos, the King of the Titans, was the last left standing, and he fought valiantly for his Earth and Children. It was, however, to no avail. Kronos was struck down, and in a moment of insatiable anger, the young Zeus leapt forth from Olympus. Zeus charged Baal with a blind courage, but his inexperience and wild nature left him vulnerable. Zeus was knocked to the frozen ground, but before Baal could end his life, Gaia appeared.

She swept Baal off his feet and far from Zeus with a mighty gust of wind. The Earth Mother then conjured whirlwinds of snow and rain, blinding and overwhelming Baal. She brought down upon him the might of the Heavens with lightning, and finally split the earth beneath his feet.

Baal fell into the cavernous abyss, which Gaia, using all her might, filled with water, rock, and earth. Zeus and his young brothers and sisters watched in quiet apprehension as a silence fell upon the world.

The ground began to quake, and Baal came howling up from his grave with a tremendous force. The Earth shook as he shot up into the Heavens. A mass of rock exploded out behind him, which would, over centuries, form to become the moon.

Baal vanished into the cosmos, and Gaia, weak from her exertions, collapsed into the snow. Zeus and his young brethren came to her aid, and it was then that they were named the new Gods of the Earth.

The Earth remained frozen for countless generations as Gaia recuperated, keeping safe the two Men and the two Women in her Garden. When she was fully healed, Gaia again blessed the Earth with sparkling oceans and lush forests. The Gods, with her aid, then helped Humanity spread and live free across the world.

The Twelve Titans, for their sacrifice, were forever immortalized in spirit, for the year would be divided into twelve cycles, and their memory would live on through the immortality of time. Gaia warned the

Gods that Baal would return, perhaps even more powerful than before, and that she may not be strong enough to defeat him again.

So it was that young Zeus sat thereupon
his throne as rightful King of Gods and Man,
Knowing too well a day would surely come
with war and death within its cruel hand.

Under the watchful eye of Zeus and the Pantheon, Humanity grew in number and spread across the lush lands of the world. The Kingdoms of Man expanded over thousands of years, and mighty cities like those of Athens, Sparta, Corinth, and Thebes were built. Humanity and the world entered an era of prosperity.

Cities of man, crafted in marble white,
Stand as testament to their mortal might,
Conquerors of both the land and the sea
gently guided by winds of Destiny.

Yet, with each passing moment, Zeus did grow weary, for he knew in his heart that Baal would again try to pry the Earth from its rightful rulers. Man, while capable in the art of war, would be reduced to nothing. These thoughts of doubt and fear, however, were remedied momentarily by a joyous occasion. Hera, wife of Zeus, bore into the world a child.

The newborn was a boy whom Zeus named Theos. The Pantheon of the Gods held a great feast in honor of the occasion, but the festivities were short lived, for on the day that Theos was born, the Earth did tremble and the skies did shake.

The Gods watched from atop Olympus as an orb of fire did descend from the sky and crash into the sea. So great was the force that a wave of immense size swept out onto the many islands and took with it the cities of Man. The Earth shook with such power that the great walls, buildings, and monuments of Humanity toppled to the ground into heaps of rubble.

Out from the sea did then rise Baal, sheathed in his armor of blackened bronze. His eyes, piercing blue, stared out onto Olympus with a fury only vengeance knew. His hand clutched the spear that struck down the mighty Titans, now thirsting for the blood of Zeus and Humanity. Baal walked across the sea and out onto land, where he called out to the Gods.

"Listen to the frantic cries of your people, to the leaders of the flock shouting in despair! Your world will be made desolate. Bow down to my power, and I will spare you death. Resist, and I shall strike you down as I did those who came before you."

So it was that the Twelve Olympians, knowing well their fate, challenged Baal. In turn, the dark God struck the ground with his spear, causing the ground to quake like thunder. Mount Olympus split, spewing molten rock and fire, reducing much of the marbled Pantheon and its halls to ruin.

Poor Hermes and Aphrodite, with all her beauty, plunged deep into the bowels of the flaming crevasse to their dooms. Hestia, the Goddess of Home, tried to flee the carnage, but the great pillars of the Pantheon came crashing down and crushed her beneath their weight. Baal, sprouting the wings of a black hawk, flew to the summit of Olympus and met the Gods in battle.

Thus began the fall of the Pantheon.

O, Mighty Poseidon, the God of Seas,
Stood firm with his Trident held high above,
Struck down so quick by
the blackened spear tip,
Life slipping from his final sigh.

Watch now Artemis, with her potent bow,
Let loose her deft arrows so quick and sharp,
But Baal pounced swiftly,
And thrust his spear into her beating heart.

Forceful Ares, the mighty God of War,
With his spear and shield did fight bravely,
Yet brushed aside with ease like resting dust,
His eyes darkened quickly like falling dusk.

See now Hades, God of the Dead below,
Fight in battle fierce,
But his staff cracked in half and life bled dry
by the spear tip that, his soul, so thus pierced.

Fly Apollo, with your chariot high,
Who charged upon the false God from beyond,
Yet came crashing down in a deathly haste
when the dark God's blow found its fatal mark.

Swing, strong Hephaestus
with your hammer strong,
Strike mightily with all your strength,
But even he was of no match
as he let free his final breath.

Deadly Athena, Goddess of the Hunt,
Swift like the summer wind upon her feet,
Was struck down like the dry leaves of the fall,
Her body crumpled.

So it was that Zeus, King of the Gods, was last left standing in defense of the world. Hera, his wife, clutched closely the infant Theos as Baal marched upon them. Zeus fought bravely, but he was cast aside, mortally wounded, and dashed against the rubble of the once mighty Pantheon. The dark God towered over the weeping Hera, who shielded her infant child. It was then that Gaia, in the form of a mighty bear, pounced upon Baal, but she was thrown aside into the rocks.

Gaia turned into her true form and tried to stop Baal with her powers, but Baal was far too strong. Gaia, weak, collapsed under the weight of her exhaustion. Hera attempted to run, but Baal cut her down, and the infant Theos was dropped onto the ground in his bundles. Zeus let out a cry of anguish, and in a rage unlike any other, he charged upon Baal wildly.

He grabbed onto the dark God, whose spear pierced Zeus through his chest. Zeus, too, dug his broken spear deep into Baal's side, and flung himself with him in his grasp into the bowels of the Earth. Baal let out a cry as they fell into the heart of Hell itself, plunging through rock and into the Palace of Hades.

They crashed down unto the black marble halls of the Underworld, where the wounded Zeus and Baal fought like animals with their hands.

Baal, keen on ending Zeus' life, strode upon him, but Zeus, with his last might, grabbed hold of Baal and screamed in a voice of thunder. Zeus flung himself into the River of Souls with Baal in his grasp, where the hands of the dead did drag them down into oblivion. Weakened and wounded, Baal could not escape, and he disappeared into the depths of the river's void.

Gaia, frail, found the strength to stand and stare down into the blackened heart of Olympus. With her last strand of power, Gaia filled the great chasm, and Baal was, for now, trapped in the depths of Hell in a tomb of stone and fire. Gaia walked over to the infant Theos, who cried out in pained confusion, and she picked him up in her arms.

He was the last living God on Earth, but was far too young to understand his place, let alone rule the world. Humanity was, for now, left Godless, and so their prosperity fell into darkness. Dry famines struck the once fertile lands, and the great cities of Man began to wage war with one another.

In the far land where the mountains withhold
the legends of Heroes long past,
Where east sea aside once bore on her back
a thousand black sails of war.

O, Rage! Sing thus of Mankind's Godless rage!
War, black and murderous, cost great,
For many souls were
thrown before Death's gate!

The world is left broken, but not destroyed.

For his safety and upbringing, Gaia took the infant God to the tiny island of Iraklia, far out in the sea. There, she left Theos under an apple tree in the center of the island's only village. Theos, crying out, was found by a fisherman named Klementos. The man carried the infant into his home, where he took him in as his own, and gave him the mortal name of Kristos.

Gaia had decided that when the time was right, she would reveal to Theos the truth of his existence. For now, the world would have to wait for their God, and hope that Baal would not escape his place in Hell until then.

-II-MAHRIA AND THE MINOTAUR-II-

~Be you therefore merciful, as your Father also is merciful~
Luke 6:36

The lands of Man were ravaged by war and deprivation for twenty years. Gaia, weak and healing, did the best she could in maintaining order. It was during this time that Theos, the son of Zeus and rightful God of Earth, lived a quiet life in the fishing village on Iraklia, which was untouched by the darkness that had fallen upon much of the world. Gaia, all awhile, kept watch over the young God as he grew in age and wisdom.

Theos helped his foster father, Klementos, with his daily fishing and common chores. As he grew, he began to realize that his strength was unlike those of other men, and so it was that the villagers often came to him for aid. Theos was seen as a blessing upon the small island, for while he was kind in heart and soul, he was an imposing youth with the build of a fine warrior. His natural skill with the sword, shield, spear, and bow was unmatched on the island, which was curious to many as he had never practiced. The locals began to tell tales of Theos' strength and character, some even suggesting that he was descendent of the Gods, but Theos paid no heed to it.

While growing up, Theos had often played with the local children, but there was one of whom he was especially fond of. She was a girl with the name Mahria, and was the daughter of a widowed fruit vendor named Agathe. Theos and Mahria often played games of strength, which was unusual for the girls, but she always held a contest of who it was that could throw a stone the furthest into the sea. Theos, at times, would lose on purpose, and Mahria would march through the village touting of her victory.

Theos had grown to find Mahria to be his closest of friends, and the two would often slip off into the night to watch the stars glisten; jewels of light sewn into the black velvet of the cosmos. They often talked of life, pondered what the world was like beyond their little island, and, at times, hinted at a mutual affection that had grown with time. Neither had the courage, however, to tell the other of their heart's desires. Theos would accompany Mahria back to her home, and he would go to bed each night with the conviction that he would tell Mahria of his feelings the next day. Yet, when the sun did rise and the next day came, Theos could not quite follow through with his self made promise.

It would seem even Gods are afflicted with the mortal hardship of shyness.

Theos' love and courage would be put to the test, however. One day before his twenty-first birthday, Theos was fixing the roof of his neighbor's home.

The mother of Mahria came rushing through the streets of the village, crying out in despair. The villagers muttered amongst themselves in curious, anxious awe, and questioned Agathe. She sobbed of her plight.

"My daughter!" she sputtered. "My daughter has gone missing! My sweet Mahria was out to pick the berries, but she was taken! Taken into the caves by a creature!"

Theos, upon hearing this, came down from the roof of his neighbor, and made it known that he would find Mahria. The island of Iraklia was riddled with caves, dark and twisting, and none had braved their mysteries. The elders told tales of a Minotaur living deep within the labyrinths of rock, but many only believed those to be stories to keep the children from entering.

Theos took the spear of his foster father, and promised to Agathe and the villagers that he would bring Mahria back by sunset. Theos set off into the wilds of Iraklia, and towards where Mahria was last seen by her mother.

After a trek that lasted a good part of the day, Theos found the entrance to a cave where the wind whispered her eerie songs. He struck a torch and entered the mouth of the rocky opening, soon being enveloped by the cold embrace of darkness. The torchlight glimmered on the damp rocks as Theos made his way deeper into the twisting caves. Soon, he heard the sound of muffled sobbing, and found that he had entered the lair of the Minotaur.

It was there he saw Mahria, unharmed, sitting in a cage of wrought metal. Upon seeing him, Mahria nearly burst into joyous laughter, but Theos hushed her, for the Minotaur lay sleeping on his bed of hay and deer skin. Theos, with his might, bent the cage open and pulled Mahria out, but it was in that moment that the Minotaur stirred awake and shrieked in anger. The creature grabbed hold a mighty axe and lunged at Theos, who fought bravely with unmatched skill.

God of Man, the art of war in his veins,
Swift with the parries of his sharpened spear,
Did scathe the Minotaur, who cried in pain,
Filling his wretched soul with biting fear.

The Minotaur, who lay upon his back with Theos' spear readied to deliver death, did cry out and beg for his life. The God, who pitied this foul creature, bid him to speak.

"Please!" uttered the Minotaur. "Spare my life, for I am hungry and weak of starvation!"

Theos, his spear still firm in his grasp, retorted.
"Why take this woman?" he asked. "Was it in your plans to eat her flesh?"

The Minotaur begged upon his knees.

"Yes! I am hungry! My stomach growls in pain! The humans of this island have stripped it bare of its food, taking it all for their own! I have never bothered them, but now, with no food, I had no choice but to prey upon them! Please, warrior, spare me my life! I learn to eat the grass and drink of mud if need be, for I do not wish to die!"

Theos, a God of great mercy, did not strike the Minotaur down. Instead, he spared his life, and even made pact with him.

"Hear me, Minotaur," he said. "Lead my friend and I back to the outside world, for you know these caves better than I. I will then promise that I shall speak to the village, and tell them of your plight, for this island belongs not to Man nor to you, but to both."

The Minotaur, disbelieving at first, agreed to help Theos and Mahria, and so he led the two through the twisted caverns and out into the light of the late afternoon sun. There, Theos gave the Minotaur his word, and the creature sulked back into the caves. Mahria and Theos made their way back into the village, where the people erupted with joy.

They celebrated and bid they drink in Theos' name, but his voice boomed and beckoned silence.

He told them of the Minotaur's plight, and how their greed of the small island's food and resources had made this creature desperate for their flesh. The villagers did not all take well to Theos' words, but his renown and character reaffirmed their faith in him, and so it was decided that they would help the Minotaur.

The villagers gathered excess bags of grain and dried fruits, and had them ferried off on the backs of mules. By sunset, the mules with their cargo had been driven to the Minotaur's cave, where they were unloaded and then led back to the village.

The twilight hour came soon with haste, and the sun had dipped below the sea. When the stars began to awaken and the sky was colored of lavender, the Minotaur came out of his lair to discover that Theos had kept his promise. The Minotaur, filled with joy and happiness, cried out into the air.

In the late hours of the night, Theos and Mahria sat under the eyes of the stars above. Mahria thanked Theos again for his bravery and laid a kiss upon his cheek. It was then that Theos, overcome by his heart, embraced Mahria and professed his love for her.

Mahria, in a fit of delighted laughter, told Theos of her own feelings, and the two were relieved to find that their affections were mutual. They then kissed and lay under the stars, talking of their future with notions of a blissful life.

All, however, was not well.

Not far from the small island of Iraklia, there lay in wait on the water three ships filled with pirates and raiders from the island of Crete. Vagabonds of crime and pillaging, the pirates had waited until nightfall to strike the small island. So, when the sun had set and darkness swathed the island in her blanket, the pirates landed upon the shore. Their party, no less than a hundred men, made towards the lone village.

Theos and Mahria, on their backs in the grass, were alerted to the cries and yells of women and men alike in the distance. They quickly got to their feet and hastened back towards the village, sprinting up to the peak of a hill. There, they saw that much of their home was in flames; the cinders drifting, licking up at the night sky.

The men of the village had taken up arms with what they could find, many stirred up from their slumber. They were no match for the hardened pirates, who began to loot the homes and drag the screeching women out into the street.

Theos, urging Mahria to stay upon the hill, ran towards the village with the wind in his every step.

Mahria watched Theos rush across the field and towards the burning village with a speed no man upon Earth could rightfully possess. For a glancing moment, in the heat of battle, she saw not a mortal man, but the soul of a God.

O' Theos, last of the Gods on Earth!
How you roar like a lion in the hunt!

Thundering across the plains with the might
of Heaven's rage within your heart!

How he grabbed the spear of a fallen friend,
Throwing it through the smoking air,
What power thus in its flight, deadly true,
Piercing the hearts of two men through!

How he grabbed the sword of a fallen friend,
Bronze edge glowing in fire's light,
What power thus in his swift swings so skilled,
A dozen more did he so kill.

The pirates, who had struck fear into the hearts of countless thousands, tasted the bitter drink of terror for the first time. Theos slew a great many of them and left their bodies mangled in his path of rage, but their numbers were great and Theos could not fight them all. He saw a group of them make way towards Mahria, and he screamed for her to run.

Mahria, seeing the pirates draw close, ran into the wilds of the island, but she grew faint in breath and her legs tired from the chase. She collapsed to the ground, and the pirates, like hungry vultures, descended upon her. Yet, before they could lay a finger on her flesh, the Minotaur, with a mighty cry, leapt forth from the bushes with his axe.

Minotaur great, with
your axe sharp and quick!
Cut the wind and flesh
with your swings!

How the bones of men crackle thus like twigs
under the might of your frenzy!

So it was that the Minotaur saved Mahria from defilement and death, the mercy of Theos repaid in full, and he urged Mahria to stay hidden in the wild. The Minotaur ran off towards the village where Theos fought bravely.

The pirates, panicked and bloodied, ran back towards their ships, but before all who remained could board the vessels, the mighty Minotaur did bound out from the night with his swinging axe. The pirates shrieked and wailed as the creature struck at them in wild arcs. Theos joined the fray, and together, the young God and the Minotaur slew the pirates to the last man.

How you sought treasures
of blood, Men of Crete!
Yet cut down by winds of Justice,
The God and Beast be Her spear and Her axe
that cast judgment upon your souls!

Theos and the Minotaur, after their victory, found it to be hollow. The flames had left much of the village a smoldering pile of ash. The paths were left strewn with the dead and wounded, and the wails of the women, mourning the loss of brave sons, fathers and brothers, trembled across the cold air.

Among the dead lay Klementos, the only father Theos knew, and he let flow his tears like a mortal man; for even Gods felt the ache of loss and death. Mahria comforted Theos with her love. Unseen by all, however, was a small, white rabbit with vivid green eyes, hiding in the bushes and watching Theos display his sorrowful humanity.

By sunrise, the dead had been accounted for and buried in ceremony by the survivors. The slain pirates, with help from the Minotaur, were thrown upon their ships, which were set afire and sunk into the sea.

Alone to their thoughts in the rising sun, Theos and Mahria sat and watched the land with a solemn weight upon their hearts. Gone were their dreams of happiness and bliss, replaced with thoughts of doubt. It was then that the white rabbit, with the green eyes, hopped forth from the tall grass and sat staring at them. Theos found this creature to be curious, for he had never seen a rabbit with eyes as these, and so in jest called out to it.

"What wish you of me, rabbit?" he asked. "I have no food for you to nibble, little one. What simple life you live. Do you mourn, as we men? When a hunter does drag your brother for his stew, do you cry and wail at the loss of him?"

The rabbit, seemingly understanding of Theos, hopped to his side and stared up at him with its green eyes. It was then, in a flash of light, that the rabbit turned into Gaia, the Earth Mother. Theos and Mahria, taken aback by this, stumbled to their feet.

"What magic is this?" uttered Mahria. "What beautiful Goddess stands before us?"

Gaia called out in a voice that soothed their aching hearts and spirits, like a mother calming a child who fears the boom of thunder. Her hair glowed in the rising sun, her robes drifted softly to the sigh of the breeze.

"I am Gaia, the Earth Mother, the spirit that which breathed life to this world and has kept watch over it long before the Gods. Theos, Son of Zeus, I have watched you grow in wisdom and heart. The time of your ascension has come, young one, for you are powerful. I have seen it."

Theos called out in disbelief.

"Son of Zeus? Theos? What do you speak of? I am the son of a dead father who gave his life for his home and family. My name is Kristos. I am a mortal who is blessed with the feelings of love and joy, yet cursed with the sting of agony. You are mistaken, great Earth Mother, for I am not who you believe me to be."

Gaia, with a smile as warm as the sun's kiss, took Theos' hand.

"You are, indeed, the son of a dead father whom named you Theos, for Mighty Zeus did give his life so that you and Humanity may live. The Gods, Theos, are dead. It is why the world has entered an era of darkness, and it is why I have come for you. You are of age to ascend the throne as Lord of Man, and to bring forth the light and bless them once again. You have much to learn and many trials ahead. A great evil is stirring, the same evil that rendered the Pantheon of Olympus empty and left decaying. I am weak, Theos. I cannot hold the fabrics of this world together much longer. You are to rebuild. You are to return hope. You are the Last God of Man."

Theos, unsure of it all, shook his head in doubt and confusion.

Mahria watched, wonderstruck, not able to comprehend such a thing.

Gaia, however, reassured them of Theos' lineage, and told them of Baal. Theos and Mahria listened to Gaia well into the afternoon hours, and she told Theos he must leave Iraklia to attend his destiny.

"Time is not our ally," spoke Gaia. "We must be swift in our decisions and actions, for I feel the stirrings of Baal. He shall erupt forth from Hell with a vengeance and hunger for destruction. We must be prepared. I will guide you, like the wind does a ship at sea, but only you can set the port to which you sail."

Mahria called out: "What destiny have I in this? If Theos be a God, I am still a mortal."

"Sweet Mahria," said Gaia. "Your place in destiny will be great, and you must have faith. For now, you will stay here on this island, safe from the dangers of the world. Theos, however, must journey to the great city of Athens, for the shadow of evil does grow with every passing hour."

Theos and Mahria, trusting in the words of the Earth Mother, accepted their fates. They went back to the village with Gaia at their side, where the villagers were in awe of her presence. There, all was explained, and the villagers who had faith in Theos trusted in the words of Gaia.

Theos bid farewell to Mahria and the others, and bid farewell to the Minotaur, who swore to keep watch over the island and its people. Theos and Gaia then boarded a small ship, and the Earth Mother guided the winds so that they sailed for the mainland.

So began the journey of the Last God.

-III-THE DARK TRINITY-III-

~Who made the world like a desert and overthrew its cities?~
Isaiah 14:17

While Theos made passage across the sea, the cities of Man on the mainland lived in the gloom of war. Perhaps the most violent and grueling of wars was that which was waged between the mighty cities of Greece and the Trojans. Hundreds upon thousands of young men, many of which who did not understand beyond the pride of their politicians the causes of their struggle, had seen their lives cut short.

Dawn, saffron light upon the Earth below,
Greet those who shine in amber bronze,
Whose spear tips in your flowing touch
so glow,
Greet those who shall last see you, Dawn.

Mothers sighing, bidding farewell to sons,
Laying upon their cheeks a kiss,
"Be brave," they say,
"May your strength not yield.
Come home with or on your shield."

Dawn, waking light upon the Earth below,
Greet those who shine in amber bronze,

Whose spear tips in your flowing touch
so glow,
Those who tomorrow shall not know.

For the living know that they will die,
But the dead know nothing,
And they have no more reward,
For the memory of them is forgotten.

O, see the restless turned to lifeless heaps.

Men, like a sheep pulled down by the lion,
Groaning, clawing at blood soaked dust,
Their souls fluttering off into the wind,
How life does Her sweet breath rescind.

Dawn, who stands witness to a battle's fore,
Count those who have thrown off their lives,
Who lay sprawled upon red soaked earth,
Dearer now to vultures than wives.

Like a flower, blooming in the Springtime,
Plucked before its beauty is full,
Never again to be seen and enjoyed,
O, to mourn youth lost in its prime.

For the living know that they will die,
But the dead know nothing,

And they have no more reward,
For the memory of them is forgotten.

Mothers weeping, faces like the sheer cliff
flowing with spring water, washing
down upon their soft cheeks to wounded cries,
Cleansing their hearts of stricken grief.

Wives sighing, bidding farewell to husbands,
Laying upon their lips a kiss,
"Be brave," they say,
"May your strength not yield.
Come home with or on your shield."

How enemy prayed against enemy,
Their prayers falling on deaf ears,
For the Halls of Olympus and Heaven
lay vacant, empty, in ruin.

So the gears of war kept in their cycles,
Fueled by the blood of brave men,
So withering the young leaves of mankind,
Generations thus left unborn.

For the living know that they will die,
But the dead know nothing,
And they have no more reward,
For the memory of them is forgotten.

While Man waged war with fellow kin, however, the depths of Hell stirred. Deep down in the darkness, Baal broke free and crawled out from the River of Souls. Weakened and thirsting for vengeance, he cried out in agony. The broken spearhead of Zeus was still imbedded deep into his side, deep and unreachable.

The pangs of pain seared across his body.

His armor of blackened bronze was chipped, his powers weakened and eroded from twenty years of captivity, but Baal stood on the banks of the river with his eyes glowing in the tinge of violent reprisal. He wandered the ancient depths of the Underworld, where the halls of Hades were long dilapidated and in ruin. Baal, with his enchantments, lit the dead torches with immortal fire, paving a path of light through the shadows. He made his way to the mighty stone doors of the palace, which he pushed open to a salutation of thick dust and grime.

Inside the darkened halls sat the empty throne of Hades. The walls of the palace, ten times the height of a normal man, were decorated with fine carvings that illustrated the torments of the Underworld. Baal gazed on these carvings, and it was then that the sound of sobbing could be heard drifting through the desolate palace. Baal followed these whispers of sadness into a chamber where there stood, in the center of the hall, a cage the size of a cottage. Within this cage sat a creature unlike any other, one of great beauty, but also of great malice.

The creature had the face and body of a beautiful woman, perfect in her shape, one that would elicit the sigh of any mortal man. Her hair was blonde and fair, flowing down upon her shoulders and back in waves of golden silk.

Yet it was here that her beauty ceased, for her eyes were as black as night, and her teeth were like those of the piranha fish when she opened her mouth. This creature, upon seeing Baal, called out to him in a voice of calm beauty, but one tinged with the hiss of a serpent.

"Who is it that walks these dead halls? Have you been sent by the Gods to end my lonely suffering?"

Baal, standing outside the cage and staring upon this fascinating creature, answered.

"No," he spoke. "Your Gods are dead."

The caged one stood, stepping towards Baal.

"Dead? Then that is why the halls have been silent for so long. Was their deaths your doing?"

Baal nodded, "Yes, it was, and I have returned to finish that which I began."

The caged one laughed, "If you truly did kill the Gods, then I hold no bitterness against you."

Baal drew closer to the cage.

"What is your name?" he asked. "Why do you sit trapped in this cage?"

"My name?" asked the caged one. "My name is Jezebel. Hera, the most jealous wife of Zeus, locked me down here into the heart of the Underworld, so that I won't give Zeus the pleasures she could not. She cursed me, as you can see, with immortal suffering, for now I thirst not for lust, but for the blood of man, woman, and child. You are no simple man either, stranger. You have the smell of a God upon you."

To this, Baal smiled and spoke:

"Because I am, and I have come to claim this world as my own. Perhaps you would be able to help me in my conquering? If I were to free you, Jezebel, shall you serve me, your True Lord, with no question of my commands? For if you serve without hesitation and with all your might, I shall see to it that you bathe in fountains of blood and drink till you are content with the sins of your gluttony."

Jezebel looked upon Baal with her dark eyes, a smile spreading across her beautiful face.

"Free me, God! Free me, and I shall aid you in your wars!"

Baal, with his might, grabbed the bars of the cage and splintered them with ease. Jezebel stepped out, free of her captivity for the first time in eons, and looked upon Baal, who placed a hand upon her face and said:

"Give, and it will be given to you."

Jezebel guided Baal through the halls of the palace, many left in ruin and decay for lack of care.

Said Jezebel, "I know of a treasure that will help you, my God, for you will need it."

The treasure, which Jezebel showed Baal, was in the armory of Hades. Inside, weapons and armor forged by the God smith Hephaestus lined the walls. In the center of the chamber, however, was a pedestal on which there lay a scabbard of wrought metal and jewels. Baal walked to this scabbard and took it from its place of rest. He pulled out the blade, and found it to be enchanted by the Gods, for the sharp edge smoldered with a blue flame.

So it was that Baal took for himself the Flaming Sword, with which he promised to subdue Man and rule over them. Baal, however, was reminded of his weakened state, as the spearhead buried beneath his flesh stung with pain. Jezebel saw this, and spoke carefully to the false God on the matter.

"You said you were trapped in the River of Souls, my God?"

"Yes," replied Baal. "For twenty years."

Jezebel proceeded with caution, not wanting to anger Baal, and said, "The River of Souls, my Lord, is a potent place. One who is trapped for so long grows weak and weary over the many years. It can turn even the most powerful of Gods into the weakest of mortals. You must be careful, for while you may still possess eternal youth, your life can be taken like any other."

Baal, who felt such weakness flow through his veins, thought for a moment before answering.

"There is no other God to fear, and I do not fear Man."

"You will need an army," said Jezebel, "for Man is powerful in the art of war."

Baal, begrudgingly accepting of his state, inquired how it was that he would raise an army. Jezebel answered.

"The loyalty of Man can be bought two ways: with riches, or with fear. There is a city, known for its indulgence, luxury, and worship of machines, called Atlantis. It is ruled by a King named Ahabikos. If we were to travel there, they will lend their armies to your cause, my God, were you to shower them with riches of gold, or threats of destruction."

Baal accepted this plan, but he questioned Jezebel as to how they would march upon this city and elicit awe with only the two of them. Jezebel led him to the Library of Hades, where tens of thousands of scrolls lined the walls. There, Jezebel told Baal of a box made of stone and bronze.

"Inside this box," said Jezebel, "is the Dragon's Tooth, harvested from the beast that once guarded the spring of Ares. If we find this box, we must take it to the surface, where we can plant the Tooth into the soil. Once planted, it will turn into a warrior, the best history has ever seen, with the strength of twenty men. It will be at your command."

And so, searching the vast library, Baal found the box. Upon taking it, Jezebel told the false God of a system of caves and tunnels that would lead them to the surface of the world through Taenarum; a peninsula in the southern lands. After traveling for seven days and seven nights, Baal and Jezebel emerged from the caves of Taenarum.

The two were greeted by the afternoon sun, and it was there, in a field, that they planted the Dragon's Tooth.

"We will need to water the tooth in the blood of a sacrifice," said Jezebel. "Wait here, my Lord, and I shall bring it."

Jezebel left, wandering along the edge of a river that led to a small village. Not wanting to draw too much attention, for she was mortal to Death's touch, she wandered into the village acting like a traveler from another land. Her beauty caught the attention of many young men, who eagerly wanted to help her.

The first man she came across was a blacksmith.

"From where does a woman of your beauty hail?" asked the blacksmith. "And why do you grace our little village?"

"I am a musician," answered Jezebel. "One that plays any instrument you so instruct me with a grace and elegance that only perfection can match. Yet, I have travelled for so long without the feel of a man upon my skin. Tell me, for I will not stay here long. Do you yearn for my touch? I know of a grove not far from here where we can delight in our sins. Will you make with me the music of lust?"

The blacksmith, who was eager to take her up on the offer, declined. He heaved a heavy sigh, and after a moment of thought, he shook his head.

"I cannot," the blacksmith said, "for I love my wife dearly. The pleasures I can have with you will be but a speck of dust compared to the pain I shall cause upon her. I am sorry, for you truly are beautiful, but I must decline your offer."

The blacksmith walked off.

The second man Jezebel came across was a hunter.

"From where does a woman of your beauty hail?" asked the hunter. "And why do you grace our little village?"

"I am a singer," answered Jezebel. "One that sings any song you so instruct me with a beauty and precision that only perfection can match. Yet, I have travelled for so long without the feel of a man upon my skin. Tell me, for I will not stay here long. Do you yearn for my touch? I know of a grove not far from here where we can delight in our sins. Will you come moan with me the songs of lust?"

The hunter, who was eager to take her up on the offer, declined. He heaved a heavy sigh, and after a moment of thought, he shook his head.

"I cannot," the hunter said, "for I love my wife dearly. The pleasures I can have with you will be but a speck of dust compared to the pain I shall cause upon her. I am sorry, for you truly are beautiful, but I must decline your offer."

The hunter walked off.

The third man Jezebel came across was a merchant.

"From where does a woman of your beauty hail?" asked the merchant. "And why do you grace our little village?"

"I am a poet," answered Jezebel. "One that can paint the beauty of the stars with words alone. Yet, I have travelled for so long without the feel of a man upon my skin. Tell me, for I will not stay here long. Do you yearn for my touch? I know of a grove not far from here where we can delight in our sins. Will you be the licentious muse of a lonely poet?"

The merchant thought for a moment.

"Well," he said, "I, too, have travelled far and wide, going long without the touch of a woman."

Jezebel, like the hawk circling her prey, walked close to him.

"Have you a wife?" she asked.

"Yes," replied the merchant, "and though she be beautiful, my work takes me far from her, and the desires of a man can only go so long without feeding.

Even when I am home she denies me my rights to her, and beating her does little to mend the matter."

Jezebel grinned and said, "Then come with me, and I shall feed the fire that burns in you."

Jezebel led the merchant far from the village and into a quiet grove in the forest. There, she grabbed the merchant and lay gentle kisses upon his neck. He was ensnared by her charms, and as he reached to grab her flesh, Jezebel opened her mouth wide with its sharp rows of teeth, and bit down into his neck.

Like the Tigress that severs her prey's neck,
The frail body going limp,
Light of life fading quick from empty eyes,
Cut the stem and the flower dies.

Jezebel, reveling in the blood of the dead merchant, dragged his corpse back to the field where Baal stood. They planted the Dragon's Tooth into the soil, and sprinkled it with the blood of the adulterer. Baal and Jezebel watched, and soon, the ground began to tremble, and the hand of a mighty warrior sprang from the earth.

It crawled forth, clawing out of his womb of soil.

Warrior, clad in his ebony bronze,
Embroidered with a Dragon's mark,
Face hidden beneath the helmet's guard,
No humanity in this heart.

The warrior stared upon Baal with eyes that glowed dull amber. The warrior, taller than Baal and wearing a full helmet plumed with a red crest, stepped forward. He spoke in a voice that sounded of a thousand voices, dark and baleful in its sound.

"Who is it," spoke the warrior, "that springs me forth from my slumber?"

Baal looked upon this warrior and answered.

"It was I. Look unto me, and be you commanded to all the ends of the Earth, for I am your God, and there is none else."

The warrior looked down onto the dark God and responded, bowing to one knee.

"Since you be my Lord, I will take command as you so wish."

"Rise, my child," spoke Baal. "Have you a name by which I will call you?"

The dark warrior lifted his head and spoke, "My name is Lucifer."

To this, Baal placed his hand upon Lucifer's shoulder, bid him rise, and said, "Then let us march, Lucifer, for the end of days is near for Humanity."

So it was that Baal, Jezebel, and Lucifer made way towards the city of Atlantis.

After a journey that lasted four days, they arrived at the gates of the city. There, the guards denied them entry, and Baal used his powers, albeit weakened, to break down the city gates. The streets were filled with terrified screams. King Ahabikos came forth from his palace, and Baal declared himself to the people of Atlantis as the one, true God. He turned the waters of the city fountains to blood, and the people were in awe and fear of his powers.

Ahabikos and his people, who lived in the comforts of luxury and indulgence, welcomed the false God so that their way of life would not be disturbed nor changed. Ahabikos had the temples of Zeus and the Olympian Gods torn down, and granted Baal control of his armies and mighty war machines of bronze: catapults, a ram, clay urns of liquid fire. Baal, in return, conquered the neighboring cities and gave their riches to Ahabikos, who in turn ruled his small kingdom in a sea of greed and extravagance.

With promises of glory and even more fortune, the armies of Atlantis blindly followed Baal. They marched upon the cities of Man, and the shadow of war cast itself across the land.

Like wheat harvested by the swinging scythe,
So were felled the Armies of Man,
Masters of their craft in War upended
by a force they could not withstand.

-IV-THE SEVEN COMMANDERS-IV-

~Where there is no guidance, a people falls ~
Proverbs 11:14

The cities of Man were ravaged by the armies of Baal. They were toppled, one after the other, and much of the world fell into darkness. The only city of refuge left for Humanity was one of the largest and strongest: the city of Athens.

The countless thousands of men, women, and children who fled the destruction of their homes all came in a great pilgrimage to Athens. It was the last bastion of hope, and peoples who once considered eachother enemies stood, side by side, as refugees. Every day, hundreds more would enter the gates of Athens, until the streets themselves were filled, end to end, with the sick and hungry. Homes that once held one family now held ten, and warehouses of grain became the sleeping quarters for children and the elderly.

The barracks, too, were filled to the brim. The remnants of defeated armies, from Thebes to Sparta, came in shambles to the gates of Athens. They told stories of the unstoppable army. Nobody knew where they had come from, or for what purpose they waged their war, but it was clear that the army of Athens needed all the help it could muster.

Within the palace, and within the royal chamber, the many seers and advisors flocked to the young warrior King, Codrus. Codrus was a ruler who, while fair in his judgments and loved by his people, was a fierce warrior with the blood of heroes flowing through his veins. When he stared out onto his city from the chamber balcony, he saw the many thousands of people that had come to his great city for protection.

The seers and advisors hounded Codrus, all trying to ascertain why this immortal army had come to ravage the land. Many believed it to be a curse from the Gods. Many more believed them to be an invading force from a land beyond their own. Regardless, each seer and each advisor had his own say.

"My King!" called one. "We must sacrifice a thousand oxen to the Gods!"

"No!" cried another. "The Gods have abandoned us!"

"No!" another would say. "The Gods are testing our faith, for they shall sweep down and stop the destruction that has ravaged our lands!"

Codrus, after many days of listening to his advisors and seers blather, had grown tired of their voices.

"Silence!" he ordered. "Grant me a moment of freedom from your words."

Codrus looked out onto his city with a heavy heart, and it was then that a messenger burst into the chambers.

"My King!" he cried. "The seven have arrived!"

Codrus looked, and in through the mighty doors strode the seven commanders. They were the last heroes of their respective armies, hailing from every corner of the known lands, now forced to set aside their politics and resentment to work as one.

The first was Amyclas, the commander of what remained of the Spartan armies, who was known for his skill with the sword and shield.

The second was Zarex, who hailed from Laconia, known for his bravery.

The third was Lamedon, who came from Sikyon, whose shield was said to be unbreakable.

The fourth was Iphito, an Amazon, who was as beautiful as she was deadly with her bow.

The fifth was Dexamenus, who called Ambracia home, renowned for his skills with the spear and javelin.

The sixth was Eioneus, who hailed from Eion, who fought with two swords; a whirlwind across the battlefield.

The seventh was Hyperbius of Thebes, who was adept and agile with both sword and spear.

So it was that the seven commanders met with King Codrus to discuss their next course of action. The cities of Man had fallen quickly to the dark army, but it was hoped that with the might of Athens, and all the remaining armies combined, victory could be attained through attrition. The Athenian army numbered 12,000. Of the other commanders, their numbers were as follows:

Amyclas commanded 2,000 Spartans.

Zarex commanded 500 from the lands of Laconia.

Lamedon commanded 750 men.

Iphito, the Amazon, had a contingent of 5,000.

Dexamenus commanded 450 men.

Eioneus commanded 600.

Hyperbius commanded 3,500 men.

The combined armies numbered 24,800 strong.

Baal's army numbered no more than 15,000, but they were thus far unstoppable.

King Codrus, wise in his reign, named Amyclas of Sparta the supreme Strategos of the combined armies. There was quarrel amongst the others with this decision, but the King quelled the fires of anger, citing that he himself was an Athenian King, but that he had just now given command of his own armies to a Spartan.

"A man can sharpen his spear, just as he can sharpen another man. Now is not the time for pride, for I am Athenian, and he is Spartan, but in the end, we drink the same water and breathe the same air. In victory, we defend the same soil. In defeat, we shall rot in it."

During these military deliberations, young Theos walked through the gates of Athens, unassuming, wearing the weary robes of a traveler. Gaia, in the form of a hawk, sat atop a tower, watching. Theos walked the busy streets, the eyes of the sick, wounded, frightened, and hungry glancing up at Him. For a moment, many kept their glance, for there was something about Theos that gave the radiance of hope. Perhaps, some thought, He was a Wiseman who had come to aid the King. Others looked upon Theos and thought Him a mighty warrior who had come to give His sword and spear to the service of Athens.

Theos walked the streets and met a guard.

"Guard," spoke Theos. "I wish to speak to the King, for I have an important message for him."

The guard, who looked upon Theos, scoffed.

"And what is it that you would have to say to the King that is of any importance? He has many duties to tend to in these troubled days, and he has no time for those who are not part of his council, especially vagrants, to seek his presence."

Theos touched the guard upon his arm.

"Listen to me," said the God, "and look upon the faces of those around you. Do you see the defeat in their eyes? The suffering? They saw their cities burn and their neighbors slain. I do not wish for you to feel the suffering and to see the horrors that these people, who flock to your city like sheep lost in a storm, have all endured. I must speak to the King."

The guard, touched by these words, led Theos to the steps of the palace. There, the palace guard commander stopped them.

"Halt!" he spoke. "What business have you in the palace?"

The guard looked to his commander and answered, "This man has come bearing news for the King."

The commander looked upon Theos with a discerning eye and said, "Has he now? The King has enough seers barking into his ear. He does not need another."

Theos stepped forth.

"I am not a seer," He spoke, "and I have not come to waste my breath. I have come to speak to the King, and if you will not guide me to him, then I shall find him myself."

Theos then walked up the palace steps. The commander shouted, and a great many guards did rush forth, their spears pointed towards Theos.

Theos looked upon them all and said, "If you truly wish to stop me from speaking to your King, then may he without love for Athens, or for all of this land, be the first to thrust his spear into me. But, if you feel that I have some hope to offer, some counsel or guidance to give, then let me pass, and have faith that your city can be saved."

The guards, upon hearing this, let Theos pass, and the young God walked into the halls of the palace. Inside, Theos made His way towards the royal chamber, from whence the voices of King Codrus and the commanders came. The chamber sentry watching shouted out to Theos, but He paid no heed. Theos opened the mighty doors.

King Codrus and the commanders looked up and saw Theos enter. Palace guardsman flocked, like flies to rotting fruit, but Codrus bellowed in his stately voice and a silence fell upon the chamber. He inquired Theos as to who He was, and how it was that the guards had granted him entry into the palace. Theos, who knew that His answer could very well educe the fury of the King and others, answered assertively. He spoke of His claim to the bloodline of Zeus, of His life on the small island of Iraklia, and how He now journeyed to Athens to aid the city and its people.

The seven commanders were in disbelief to these claims. Some laughed, others showed their outrage, and some remained silent in their thoughts.

"You claim to be a Son of Zeus?" cried Dexamenus of Ambracia. "This is contemptible! You stride into the palace of Athens, seek the presence of King Codrus, and claim yourself a God? The guards should have you thrown into the very depths of the dungeons below so that your claims may decay with you! I say, Theos, if you truly are the son of Zeus, why do you not march up to Olympus and beg of your father to aid us in our time of need?!"

"I cannot," answered Theos, "for Zeus is dead."

A silence fell upon the air. Codrus stared upon Theos, who quietly told the King of how Gaia, the Earth Mother, had rescued Him.

He told them of Baal, the false God, who had come to conquer the world, and who, as they spoke, marched an army towards Athens. Dexamenus, still disbelieving, drew his sword and announced:

"If you truly are a God, then why do we not test your immortality?"

Codrus called for calm, but the murmurs of discontent spread like fire across the dry brush. Before their tempers reached its apex, however, Gaia, in the form of hawk, flew in from the balcony. All eyes followed her flight, and the hawk perched upon the throne of Codrus. There, in a brilliant flash of light, Gaia took her true form; her robes billowing in the whimpering breeze.

The King and the seven commanders stared upon her in awe, their disbelief as great as their wonder. She stepped forward, and in her voice of music, quelled their anger. She doused their curiosity with her answers, and when she was finished, she looked to Theos.

"Theos, Son of Zeus," she spoke. "You are truly the last hope for Mankind. Only you have the power to stop Baal and his army of followers.

Amyclas shook his head.

"But Gaia," said the Spartan, "you tell us that this Baal, this false God, wiped out our Pantheon. It now does lay in ruin, and our prayers fall upon deaf ears.

Twelve Gods could not defeat this darkness. What have we to believe and hope that one God, young and unproven, will succeed?"

Gaia placed a hand upon Amyclas and answered, "You must have faith in Him, for He is all that is left."

Gaia then turned to Theos and told Him of His trials to come.

"Theos, you are skilled in the art of war, for it was passed down into your blood, but you will not be able to stop Baal as you are now. You must acquire the Five Heroic Treasures, and only then, will you have the power and knowledge with which to defeat Baal and all who follow him. The journey will take you to the ends of the known world and back. It will take you through dangers that no mortal has ever faced. Your journey will take six days, but on the sixth day, you shall return, and shall return triumphant."

To this, Codrus spoke.

"Six days?" he asked. "Corinth and Sparta fell to Baal within one. How can we hold Athens for six days without the aid of a God at our side? How can we possibly attain victory?"

Gaia turned to the warrior King, soothing his anxiety with her motherly voice.

"You must hold the city for six days, King Codrus. There will be much sacrifice, and the streets will flow with tears of mothers, but Theos, the True God, shall return upon the sixth day so that your mourning and sacrifice shall not be in vain. Theos must leave by nightfall, for Baal's army marches quick, and I fear he shall arrive in one day's time."

So it was decided that Theos would go on His venture of six days to acquire the Five Heroic Treasures, and during this time, the seven commanders would lead their army and hold Athens until His return. Theos was given the finest horse in Athens, given a spear, helm, and armor from the royal armory, and Gaia met Him outside the gates of Athens to give her final instructions.

"I shall stay here and do what I can, weak as I am," said Gaia. "You must be swift in your journey."

And so Gaia told Theos of the Five Heroic Treasures.

The first was the winged horse, Pegasus, who lived in a sacred grove on the coast of Epirus, marked by a marble pillar.

The second was the Aegis, a set of armor said to be impenetrable, located in Mycenae, north of Athens.

The third treasure was the Spear of Achilles, the weapon of the great hero of the Trojan War, located far to the north on the small island of Lefkos.

The fourth was the Sword of Peleus, the father of Achilles, located on the small island of Ikos in the eastern sea.

The fifth and final treasure was the Shield of Ajax, said to be unbreakable, located on the island of Kypros, near the city of Salamis far to the east.

Theos, hearing this, prepared Himself for His journey and His trials. He looked to Gaia with a heavy heart, for His thoughts wandered, and He spoke softly.

"Gaia," said Theos. "What if I do not return in six days time?"

To this, Gaia smiled, and placed a hand upon the young God's face, saying, "Listen to me well, son of Zeus, for I shall say this only once: Humanity cannot have faith in a God who does not have faith in Himself."

Theos thought on these words, and Gaia bid Him farewell. And so, the last God rode forth on His horse, the late afternoon sun shining down upon Him, and the city of Athens would eagerly await His return.

-V-ODYSSEIA-V-

~Train up a child in the way he should go; even when he is old he will not depart from it~
Proverbs 22:6

Speak, Memory:

Speak of the God who embarked on His quest
to claim His Kingdom of Heaven and Earth.
Sing of His journey across the vast lands,
Sing of Him who was the last hope of Man.

So began the First Day of His voyage,
Trials thus to test His heart and courage.

Epirus, land graced by Beauty's soft touch,
With canyons carved deep and its rivers wide,
Rugged and weathered by the songs of wind,
Trees bearing wisdom handed down by Time.

Mountains, cloaked in snow
from the winter winds,
Melting under breath
of the warm East breeze,
The rivers swell in their channels once parched.

In the awe of these immortal peaks tall,
In a valley lush and untouched by Man,

Was a grove where the
Nymphs did sing and dance,
Caretakers of their sheltered home and land.

By a pond as clear as the summer sky,
Its beauty serene in a sheltered bliss,
Sat the Pegasus in beauty, pristine,
The Nymphs bathing in sunlight's gentle kiss.

Theos, Last God of Man and Heaven, rode to the edge of this veiled and secluded land. He saw the old marble pillar in the far distance, like a beacon, protruding forth from the canopy. Theos let free His weary horse from his service, for the forest was thick and could be traveled only by foot. The young God walked into the calm forest, and made way towards the pillar.

The Nymphs thus did hear
His approach draw near,
And scattered like fireflies into dawn.
They hid in the brush,
So watching in hush,
And the God's manly beauty they all fawned.

Theos stepped out near the pond that shined
like a perfect blanket of idle glass,
The Pegasus stirring from quiet rest.

The Nymphs, fearing of this stranger's intentions, revealed themselves, and Theos was taken aback by their surprise and beauty.

"Stop, stranger!" they called. "From where do you come? No man has ever graced our lands!"

Theos spoke, calm in His presence, assuring the Nymphs that He did not come to harm them. The young God told His tale to the Nymphs, who listened like children to the poet, frightened by the evil that they now knew existed beyond their sanctuary.

The Nymphs, entrusted with the Pegasus, told Theos they would gladly let Him take the mythical horse, but that they would only grant Him the saddle needed to control Pegasus if He helped them. Theos agreed, and the Nymphs told Theos of their plight.

A centaur named Eurytion lived in the depths of a cavern to the west. Eurytion, they explained, was a creature, half man, half horse, which would prey on the nubile Nymphs at night. If Theos were to slay him, they would grant the saddle of Pegasus. The young God agreed to this, and He set forth into the woods towards the cavern.

A mouth into the darkness of the Earth,
Vines like snakes ensnared
around sharpened rocks,
Wind howling Her song
of ghostly echoes.

There stood the last God.

Theos stared into the emptiness, clutching His spear. He shouted into the void, His voice like thunder.

"Eurytion! Come forth from your veil of darkness, for I am a God of great mercy, but also one of equal severity to those who dare harm the innocent of this sacred grove. Come forth, and we may talk as men!"

Theos was answered with silence, and the cave whispered of the wind. He was set to enter, but in that instant, Eurytion leapt from the shadows, armed with sword and spear. He hissed and howled, striking at Theos with a maddened rage.

Like a moth drawn to flame in the deep night,
So are such beasts drawn
to both blood and war,
Thirsting for the scent of fear and battle,
The clang of bronze upon bronze their music.

Theos parried the strikes of the raging Eurytion, His Godly skills no match for the mortal creature. It waned in breath, and Theos struck him down. The centaur fell into the dirt, flailing like a beached fish, and begged for mercy.

"Please!" it cried. "Spare me my life, warrior!"

To this, Theos answered.

"Leave the grove to its peace," spoke the God, "for if you harm another Nymph of this place, I shall return, and your debt will be paid in full to the tip of my spear."

Eurytion scampered to his feet.

"Yes!" he answered. "Yes! You have my word!"

In that moment, Eurytion grabbed his dropped spear and lunged for the unsuspecting Theos. The God, however, was quick in His reflexes, and He thrust His spear into the neck of Eurytion. As life slipped from the creature's eyes, Theos spoke.

"I shall not kill the innocent and righteous, but I shall also not acquit the wicked."

And so the God grew with the knowledge of Integrity.

Eurytion crumpled into a heap, left to be taken by the earth, and Theos made way back to the sacred pond and the Nymphs. There, He told them that the centaur was no more, and they rejoiced in their newfound safety. As promised, they presented to Theos the saddle of Pegasus. The winged horse, accepting of her new master, let Theos place the saddle upon her. He sat upon the back of Pegasus, and bid the Nymphs farewell.

He soared off into the air with Pegasus, the sun setting below the horizon, the sky turning gold and beckoning the stars to awaken. Theos rode into the night, knowing well His journey and trials had only just now begun.

So ended the First Day.

Speak, Memory:
Speak of the God who embarked on His quest
to claim His Kingdom of Heaven and Earth.
Sing of His journey across the vast lands,
Sing of Him who was the last hope of Man.

So began the Second Day of voyage,
Trials thus to test His heart and courage.

Mycenae, city built by the ancients,
Now only ruins of memory lost,
Your mighty walls and towers toppled down,
Your streets snaking, empty, walked by spirits.

Monuments of stone
wrapped by ancient vines
that coil around,
The rain falling from the Heavens above,
Washing the memory of your glory.

Theos landed before the ruins of Mycenae in the late night. He bid the Pegasus to await His return, and tied the reigns to a lone tree by the collapsed walls. Theos, spear in hand, walked into the lonely streets of the ancient city. The stars, witnesses of the first to set foot in Mycenae for over two centuries, glowed above and gave light to the lifeless marble below.

Theos walked carefully, for He sensed that He was not alone. It was then, from the ruins, that the voice of an old man carried in the wind.

"I feel the warmth of life enter my city of empty marble," spoke the voice. "I sense great purpose in you, as I also sense the blood of Gods in your veins. Follow…Follow…"

Theos watched as ancient torches burst aflame, leading a path into the heart of the ancient city. The young God followed this path of light, leading Him towards a ruined temple. The voice of the old man drifted in the breeze again.

"Enter…enter…"

Holding firm His spear, Theos walked into the dilapidated temple. Inside, mighty pillars lay toppled and the moonlight shined in beams from holes in the roof. The strange voice beckoned once more.

"Follow..follow.."

A single torch then lit, leading to a staircase that led deep under the temple. Theos passed through the cobwebs built over lost decades, descending into the unknown below. As the God reached the bottom of the stairwell, the chamber in which He stood lit up with torches that burned blue. In the center of this chamber lay a marble tomb, onto which a single ray of moonlight from a crack far above did fall.

A breeze, mystical in nature, fluttered the torch flames, and the voice of the old man called once more from the darkness.

"You have come for my armor, young one. The Aegis, impenetrable and unbreakable, passed down to Perseus by the Gods in ancient times. Open the tomb, for the worthy may don the Aegis as their own."

Theos moved to this marble sarcophagus, and with Godly might, pushed off the lid to a cloud of dust. Inside was the skeletal body of Perseus, the ancient Hero, wearing the mystical and legendary Aegis. The plumed helmet, the greaves, and the cuirass shined as if polished new. Theos stared in awe, but as He did, the bony hands of Perseus reached up, and his eyes glowed with a blue flame.

Hero of Ancients, rise from your slumber,
Give trial to the young God before you!
May He now prove His worth and His courage
as rightful heir to throne of Olympus!

Theos staggered back, raising His spear, as the skeletal form of Perseus leapt from its resting place.
This warrior of bone and dust fought deftly, but Theos did knock him unto the walls of marble. The skeleton warrior burst into powder, disintegrating into the air and swept away in a breeze.

The torches fluttered, and the voice of the old man drifted forth from the corners of the chamber, laughing.

"You are worthy, young one. You are Him who I was charged with to await. Now, that you have come, this armor, the Aegis, is yours. May it protect you as it did once me."

The young God, upon hearing this, took the armor for Himself. He put on the greaves, the helm, and the cuirass.

And so the God grew with the knowledge of Honor.

God of Man, shine in your bronze of legends,
See how the moonlight does kiss your helmet,
Glowing to Her touch,
Shining in Her awe.
A beacon of hope in this time of war.

Theos made His way out of the ruined temple, walking through the empty streets of Mycenae. The morning had come, the sky a deep purple as the early rays of the sun awakened. Theos made way to Pegasus and untied her. He mounted the saddle, and flew off into the growing fog of the newborn day.

He set sight on the island of Lefkos, far to the north, where He would find the Spear of Achilles.

So ended the Second Day.

Speak, Memory:
Speak of the God who embarked on His quest
to claim His Kingdom of Heaven and Earth.
Sing of His journey across the vast lands,
Sing of Him who was the last hope of Man.

So began the Third Day of voyage,
Trials thus to test His heart and courage.

Lefkos, island north in the wild lands,
Secrets of darkness in your labyrinths,
A place no man has walked for centuries,
The breath of eternal winter around.

So began the Third Day.

The small island of Lefkos sat in a sea of gray, the clouds around weeping of snow as the winds blinded out all sight with a wintered flurry. Theos set Pegasus down onto the desolate island, on which there stood a single temple. The young God rode Pegasus up the steps and into the empty hall. There, in flickering torchlight, Theos tied Pegasus to a pillar.

"Is there anyone here?" He bellowed. "A caretaker of this temple?"

Theos was answered with silence.

With spear in hand, He walked deeper into the temple, where He saw a priestess, in her robes, standing before a statue of Achilles. Theos called out to her, but she did not respond to His calls. He moved closer and touched the priestess on the shoulder.

It was then Theos realized that the young priestess was turned to stone, her gaze of horror frozen for all time to remember. The young God looked and saw others just like her, set in stone and immobile. Theos clutched His spear, sensing the evil that had perverted this place of reverence, and stared into the shadowed corners of the temple.

The sounds of hissing emanated forth from the darkness, and in that instant, a Gorgon leapt from the void, screeching and wailing.

With the face and body of a woman,
Hair, a hundred serpents hissing their tongues,
Eyes glowing red with a thirsting fury
that knows no bounds to its awful craving.

The Gorgon, with her gaze, could turn any man or beast to stone, but Theos, being a God, was immune to such affect. The Gorgon wailed and screamed, striking at Theos, who parried her blows. They fought within the halls of the temple until the Gorgon waned of breath. In a mighty throw, Theos sent His spear flying through the air, and it pierced through the Gorgon's head.

The serpents upon her head ceased in their hissing as they went limp, and her body slumped to the marble floor. The Gorgon turned to stone, and with her death, the priestess and the others under her curse were lifted from it.

Theos watched as the temple's caretakers had the warmth of life returned to them. The priestess gave a laugh of joy and relief, tears swelling in her eyes. She looked to Theos and cried out:

"Warrior! You have freed us from our doom! That vile creature had come in the night, from where we do not know, and I thought that we were fated to a slow death. Thank the Gods you came!"

Theos, who was pleased that He had helped these innocents, told His tale to the priestess and the others. They looked on in awe and wonder, and when it was all said, the priestess bowed down her head to the young God and proclaimed:

"The treasure you seek is here, for this is the Temple of Achilles, dedicated to the memory of the great hero. Here he lies for history to remember, and so, too, does the spear lay in rest here."

The priestess then showed Theos the statue of Achilles, and in its hand was clutched the bronze and gold spear. The priestess had it taken down and handed to Theos, who thanked her for aiding Him in His journey. The caretakers of the temple, however, felt indebted to the young God, but to this, Theos spoke.

"The wicked borrows but does not pay back, but the righteous is generous and gives."

And so the God grew with the knowledge of Rectitude.

Theos, with the Spear of Achilles in His hand, mounted Pegasus. The priestess and the others bid Him farewell, and the young God flew off into the snowy night. He set journey for the island of Ikos, to find the sword of Peleus.

So ended the Third Day.

Speak, Memory:
Speak of the God who embarked on His quest
to claim His Kingdom of Heaven and Earth.
Sing of His journey across the vast lands,
Sing of Him who was the last hope of Man.

So began the Fourth Day of voyage,
Trials thus to test His heart and courage.

Ikos, island far in the eastern sea,
With your pebbled beaches and calm waters,
A refuge from a world of chaos,
But the shadows of darkness stretch quickly.

So began the Fourth Day.

The island of Ikos was once a calm paradise in the eastern sea. Its small towns, known for their almonds and olives, had been, for a long while, spared of pirates and the famines that had struck much of the world. Yet, like many things in the world, this peace would not last, and it was only a matter of time before pirates and conquerors would come to the island with a thirst for riches and women.

Led by a mighty warrior named Goliakos, the raiders had come quickly and suddenly. Those who resisted them were killed, and those who survived were enslaved. Soon, many of the villages on Ikos were under the control of Goliakos, and so, too, were its riches his. Farmers found that they were now slaves upon their own land, and the brave men and women who dared rebel found their insurgency short lived.

One place, the town of Patitiri, had yet to be conquered by Goliakos. The people looked to their young leader, Dauid, for courage and leadership. The militia of Patitiri was small and ill equipped, but Dauid was a man filled with confidence as he was with valor.

So it was that when Theos came from the sky upon Pegasus, the people of Patitiri were in awe and felt great hope. The young God, seen with the Spear of Achilles and the Aegis, was looked at as the one who would solve the woes of the island.

Dauid welcomed Him to his humble little palace, where Theos told the ruler of His journey, the war, and His seeking of the Sword of Peleus. Dauid, however, had grim news for Theos, for the sword had been taken by Goliakos when he looted the Temple of Peleus. It became clear that the only way to retrieve the sword would be to free the island of its subjugation.

Dauid told Theos of where Goliakos had built a small outpost, the seat of his rule, and how to reach it. Having faith in the young God, Dauid had the militia mustered, and they marched. The sun had reached its late afternoon peak when the sentries of Goliakos spotted the approaching militia, and so Goliakos himself was summoned from his tent. Upon seeing the small contingent, he laughed heartily and spotted Dauid upon a horse. Goliakos called to him from across the plains.

"Dauid, you young fool! Have you finally come to die?"

To this, Dauid drew his sword, but Theos calmed his tempered blood with His touch. Theos, with His winged horse, galloped to the forefront, where the men of Goliakos gasped as they mustered their weapons and armor. Goliakos himself was in awe of this sight, for Theos shined in His godly bronze and gold.

The young God called out to Goliakos.

"Conqueror! I stand here as the rightful God of Man, and give you warning that if you do not leave this island, I will see to it that its soil is sodden with the blood of you and your men. You are thieves, rapists, and cowards, and I will have no such company praying and worshipping me, for in doing so, you defile my name and my rightful throne on Olympus. As God, this island is mine, these people are mine, and I will ask of you this only once: let my people go."

To this, Goliakos responded not with words, but with a cry that gave order for his archers to fire and soldiers to charge. The small militia of Dauid stood firm, and Theos charged forth with Pegasus.

So began the battle.

Leaves,
So dry and crumpled from the frigid winds,
Blowing off to the ends of the world
to their sad, lonely deaths and hollow ends.
So were felled the men of Goliakos
by the young God and His agile strikes.

Theos, with his Godly might, was unstoppable upon the field of battle, and the raiders lost heart at the sight of Him. Goliakos, however, with his great stature and strength, flung his spear at Dauid, striking his horse, and knocking the young leader to the ground. Theos, lost in the heat of battle, could not come to Dauid's aid, and so the young warrior got to his feet and confronted the mighty Goliakos.

Like the fish that swims against the current,
Or the bird flapping in a hailstorm,
The fates and odds so against him this day,
A pebble standing in the mountain's shade.

So, too, was Dauid in his fight against Goliakos, who towered over him with his brute strength. Yet, where Goliakos was strong and powerful, Dauid was quick with his feet and wit. It was then, in a moment where Goliakos was caught off guard, Dauid flung his spear, and it pierced Goliakos in between the eyes.

His body went limp, life left his eyes, and he slumped onto the bloodied field. The raiders cried out, for their leader was now dead, and those who still lived lay their weapons down and begged for mercy.

Dauid ordered that the raiders board their ships, and so, at sword point, the surviving raiders were shepherded like animals onto a vessel. It was then that Dauid ordered that the ship be set afire, and so it was.

Like ants scurrying in their deep tunnels
when smoke fills every passage and corner,
So, too, did the thieves and rapists scramble
as the licking flames ensnared their damned souls.

Theos watched, no pity in his heart, as Dauid did say to Him:

"Any who do wrong will be paid back for the wrong he has done, and there is no partiality."

And so the God grew with the knowledge of Justice.

With the island of Ikos free of its captivity, the militia searched the treasure troves of the dead Goliakos, and found the Sword of Peleus. Dauid had it presented to Theos, who took the sword with honor and gratitude. The scabbard, bronze and encrusted with jewels, was a beauty to behold, and the young God tied it to His belt. Theos, then, to an uproar of applause and gratefulness from the people of Ikos, took to the back of Pegasus and flew off into the setting sun.

So ended the Fourth Day.

Speak, Memory:
Speak of the God who embarked on His quest
to claim His Kingdom of Heaven and Earth.

Sing of His journey across the vast lands,
Sing of Him who was the last hope of Man.

So began the Fifth Day of voyage,
Trials thus to test His heart and courage.

Kypros, island far in the eastern sea,
With your exotic beasts and mountains tall,
The city of Salamis on your shore,
So glistening white with its marble walls.

So began the Fifth Day.

Theos would arrive onto the island of Kypros, landing near the city of Salamis in search of the Shield of Ajax. The young God knew He must hurry, for it was already the fifth day of journey. Any setback, He feared, would make it impossible for Him to return upon the Sixth Day.

When He arrived, glistening in the Aegis with the Spear of Achilles in hand, the people of Salamis were in panic and fear. Theos, who at first thought that it was Him that they feared, realized that the city was being ravaged by a Manticore.

The beast, with the body of a lion, the tail of a scorpion, and the giant wings of a bat, stormed through the streets, devouring people whole. Its cries, which rang across the air like a trumpet, were so loud and deafening that people keeled over in pain. Theos took flight with Pegasus and flew over the beast, throwing down His spear, straight and true.

Lightning,
Spear tip tearing down through the air
with a boom that shook the earth and Heavens,
Striking the beast below with a force great
that no earthly creature could so withstand.

So was the Manticore struck!

The Spear of Achilles smoldered through the Manticore's hide, which roared in agonizing pain. It took flight, the spear stuck deep within its back, and chased Theos through the sky. The young God drew the Sword of Peleus and, with a deft leap, flung Himself from Pegasus and onto the Manticore. There, He stabbed the creature a great many times and severed one of its wings. The Manticore writhed in pain wildly, and as it plummeted towards the ground below, Theos was hurled from its back. Pegasus came from the clouds in a great haste and flew to Theos' aid, coming up from under Him and catching the young God upon her back.

The Manticore crashed into the city streets, where it lay dead, and the people of Salamis rejoiced. Theos came and landed near the dead creature, fetching the Spear of Achilles from its hide, and the leaders of Salamis were in awe of Him and His sight. Theos told them of His journey, and His seeking of the Shield of Ajax. The leaders and elders of Salamis told Theos that the shield was hidden deep in the Sanctuary of Ajax, in the snowy Troodos Mountains on the western edge of the island. They feared, however, that some evil had made home in the sanctuary, for its caretakers and priests had not been seen or heard of for weeks.

Theos, then, made quick journey to the Troodos Mountains, where the windswept snow did blind all vision. There, He spotted the Sanctuary of Ajax, marked by a giant fire in a marble cistern. Theos landed Pegasus in this spot, and left her there in the warmth of the fire. Theos walked towards the sanctuary, where He felt the presence of a darkness, as the snow drifted down from the darkened clouds above.

Theos called out, but there was no answer to be heard, and only the wind howled across the empty halls. The young God, making way into the desolate sanctuary, soon saw the frozen corpses of those who once cared for this now bleak place. It was then, from the darkness, there came the sound of fluttering wings and talons tapping against stone floors. Theos stared into the shadows, and soon, He saw the glowing eyes of the beasts that had desecrated this sacred place.

In a screeching flurry, a flock of Harpies bolted out from the dark; beasts with the bodies of birds and the heads of hideous, old women.

Like hornets in a fury of anger
descending upon a fool in quick rage,
Or vultures flocking to corpses of men
whom lay on the barren fields of War.

So did the Harpies entangle Theos. The young God, with His Godly tools of War, did strike and parry at the Harpies, whose talons broke and cracked against the Aegis. Soon, the snow blanketed earth was soaked with their blood, and the Harpies that remained flew off into the forests around in a terrified frenzy. When calm had returned, Theos sheathed His blade, retrieved His spear, and fetched a sturdy tree branch. He set it aflame in the fires of the cistern, and with this torch, set foot into the empty Sanctuary of Ajax.

Theos ventured deep into the chambers of the sanctuary. It was there, in the very center, that He saw the marble tomb of Ajax. Upon this tomb stood a mighty statue of the fabled hero, and in its hand, was the Shield of Ajax. Theos stared in awe at this wonder, and it was then that a cold breeze did blow and a man's voice did drift with it.

"You are Him that seeks my shield. Come, Hero of Gods, and take the shield as your own—if you can."

With those words, the statue of Ajax came to life, and threw its marble spear at the young God. Theos leapt away, and the spear shattered against the marble wall. The statue, mighty in its pose, cracked the floors with every step. Theos readied himself.

Like two wolves circling eachother round,
Snarling and snapping their teeth with rage
that send shivers down
even brave men's spines,
Waiting for their moment to leap and strike,
Their eyes burning with a focused fury.

So Theos fought with the possessed statue, agile on His feet and quick with His strike. Soon, Theos shattered the marble limbs with His blows, and it was not long before the statue toppled and shattered into a thousand shards. In the heap that lay before Him, the Shield of Ajax shined in its gold and bronze.

Theos took the shield as His own, and made His way out of the sanctuary.

And so the God grew with the knowledge of Courage.

Theos rushed across the empty courtyard and took to the back of Pegasus. With the treasures now in His possession, the young God hurried off towards Athens. Knowing well His journey would take one day to complete, Theos hoped no misfortune would befall Him so that He may return in time upon the Sixth Day.

Theos took to the skies.

Speak, Memory:
Speak of the God who embarked on His quest
to claim His Kingdom of Heaven and Earth.
Sing of His journey across the vast lands,
Sing of Him who was the last hope of Man.

So ended the Fifth Day.

-VI-THE WAR OF HEROES-VI-

~Blessed be the Lord, my rock, who trains my hands for war~

Psalms 144:1

While Theos traveled to the far reaches of the world, the commanders of Athens readied their men for the trials ahead. While many doubted that they could hold the city for six days, Amyclas, the Spartan leader and appointed Strategos of the combined armies, took heart in the words of Gaia and believed it possible. King Codrus, too, had faith in the young God and His return, and so it was that he and Amyclas discussed their strategies of war.

So began the First Day.

On the morning that Theos departed, more refugees arrived in the wake of the destruction of their homes. Among them was Mahria, whom Gaia recognized, watching her from the balcony of the royal palace. Gaia summoned that guards bring the young woman to her. Mahria, who was frightened and tired, was escorted to the palace, and it was there that Gaia bid her welcome.

The King, who asked of the woman, was told by Gaia that she was to play an important role in the destiny of the world, and that she was to be protected. Trusting these words, Codrus had Mahria taken to the royal bed chambers deep in the palace, where she could rest from her travels.

It was there, in the bed chambers, that Gaia questioned Mahria of her journey, who solemnly told of how the island of Iraklia had fallen into sudden famine. Pirates, too, had returned, and she told of how the Minotaur had made good of his promise, for he had sacrificed himself so that she and a handful of others may escape. Mahria, then, asked Gaia of Theos, and she told her of His journey and return in six days. To this, the Mahria fretted, as one who yearns to see her friend and lover, and it was then that Gaia sensed it.

"Mahria," spoke the Earth Mother. "I can feel the warmth of life within you."

"What do you mean, Gaia?" asked Mahria.

To this, Gaia smiled and placed a hand upon Mahria's stomach. So she spoke:

"A seed of a child grows within you, Mahria. No more than a few weeks planted and watered!"

Mahria, then, admitted quickly to Gaia that on the night the village was attacked, and Theos bravely defended their home, she did lay with Him and profess her love. It was as Gaia thought, and she took Mahria's hand to say:

"Mahria, this news is joyous, for the child, then, has the blood of a God, and the Pantheon can and shall be rebuilt. You must come to no harm during these troubling days, and I will see to it that you—and your child—are kept safe from the dangers to come."

King Codrus, who was told this news, saw to it that the Royal Guard kept watch over the room. Mahria rested, and Gaia stood on the balcony, overlooking the overflowing city of Athens. As the sun traversed the sky, Amyclas and the others planned the defense of the city. The sun set, the stars awoke from their slumber, and the sentries kept watch over the night.

So ended the First Day, and gave light to the Second.

When morning came, sentries from the western walls cried out. One such sentry ran to the main barracks, where Codrus, Amyclas, and the others planned their defense. There he stood, panting, catching his breath, before finally uttering, wide eyed:

"Movement in the forests to the west! The army approaches!"

Amyclas quickly ordered the others to muster their troops. Iphito, the Amazon, had her warriors stationed atop the walls, from whence they could rain down their arrows in a hail of wood and bronze. Amyclas and the other commanders led their men out onto the field beyond the western wall, taking their battle formations, and waited.

King Codrus, high atop the wall, watched as the forest in the distance rustled. The ground trembled, and soon, out marched the army of Baal. These men, traitorous pillagers of their own world driven by greed, laid their hungry eyes upon Athens. Baal himself, the false, dark God, walked in the rear of his army. Jezebel acted as his advisor, and Lucifer acted as both his guard and general.

The men of Atlantis halted. Baal looked out to the joint armies of Athens.

Stillness,
Two mountains staring across a valley,
Standing tall and powerful in stature.
A Lion snarling at his reflection
in a still pond of crystal clear water.

So, too, stood the two mighty armies in silence.

Baal called out.

"I have wiped out many cities, devastating their fortress walls and towers. They are now deserted. Their streets are in silent ruin. Kneel. Throw down your weapons. Worship me, and I shall show you that I, too, can be merciful to those who once sought to do me harm."

King Codrus cried out from atop the walls:

"We have seen your acts of mercy. The tears of mothers and wives are testament to it, and the vultures are witnesses of it. I bid you come and claim this city. I dare you to pry it from our swords and shields. You have asked the wrong people for your worship, for not even in the embers of our dying breaths shall we utter a prayer in your name."

And with that, Amyclas below hollered, and the Amazons atop the walls let loose their arrows.

So began the War of Heroes.

Rain,
Piercing shards of bronze
and wood searing down
unto the heads of armored men below,
Their hides of metal and leather no use
to the swift points of the Amazon's bows.

Charging,
With a cry that split the clouds in Heaven,
Baal let roar his orders across the ranks,
The treacherous army of Atlantis
running with their swords
and spears pointing sharp at their fellow Man.

Thundering,
Shining bronze clanging against shining bronze,
Two waves of flesh and metal colliding
on the fields outside of Athens great.
Two walls of shields grinding together,
The noise so deafening in its clamor.

Fearless,
So were the Seven Commanders in fight,
Leading far in the forefront with their cries
that brought courage to the weak in spirit,
Like rain that gives drink to the parched flower
on a dry, hot day.

Daring,
Dexamenus, one of Ambracia,
Leading forth his men deep into the lines
of the enemy army before them,
Cut through the men of Atlantis quickly,
Setting his sights on mighty Lucifer
like a hawk hungry in his nimble hunt,
Eyes sharp like the owl in darkest night.

Soaring,
Dexamenus so let fly his sharp spear,
Elevated over the heads of men
and aimed towards the towering Lucifer.
The great warrior in his blackened bronze
caught the flying spear in his metal grasp,
Crushing the tip and splintering the shaft,
Dexamenus thus left stunned and aghast.

Leaping,
So did Lucifer with spear and shield
lunge upon Dexamenus with hot rage,

The spear tip glancing the hero's helmet,
Carving into the bronze like a river
that cuts through rock and whittles a valley.
Dexamenus was brave in his fighting,
But his breath waned and muscles ached.
His sword strikes grew tired.
His shield dropped.
He fell.
Death.

Lucifer struck down Dexamenus, but the men of Atlantis had grown tired, and these followers of Baal started to fall back. The dark God himself rose to join the fight, but the pangs of pain from his old wounds and past captivity once again reminded him of his weakened state. Baal bellowed and ordered the army to regroup, and as he did so, the dark God saw Gaia staring down upon him from the balcony of the royal palace in the heart of Athens. They were far apart, but the two looked deep into the eyes of the other, and what it was that they saw was to be known only by them.

The army of Atlantis, led by Lucifer, retreated from the walls of Athens, and quickly, Amyclas ordered the shepherding of the wounded. He and Zarex, the hero of Laconia, went and gathered the fallen Dexamenus. The Amazons kept close watch over the field, strewn with countless dead, and a calm fell over the air as Amyclas ordered the armies back into the safety of the city.

So ended the Second Day.

As the sun set and darkness came, Amyclas ordered Iphito and her Amazons to keep watch during the night. The camps and fires of Baal's army dotted the horizon, spheres of flame dancing far in the distance as omens of the coming morning.

So, too, did Baal watch the torches high on the walls of Athens, trying to hide the pain of his past battle wounds. Late in the night, Jezebel approached the false God in his tent.

"My Lord. You must be careful, for it would seem your wounds are worse than first thought. Yet, even weakened, these mortals should be no match for you. Have you not conquered countless other worlds? Vanquished countless other Gods?"

To this, Baal grew angry, but he, too, understood that this world was different, and that this battle was unlike others he had fought.

So spoke Baal:

"Gaia, this world's Spirit Mother, bested me once before. She is weaker now, but as am I, and it is her that I am wary of. Yet, there is something else. These people…they are different. Different from others I have conquered. They believe that they can defeat me. They have *faith*. As long as they have faith, and blind belief in victory, they will fight with full hearts and high spirits."

"Then it is simple, my Lord," spoke Jezebel. "We break their faith, rip out the spine that is their spirit, and then they shall cower in the shadows of our victory."

Baal thought, and thus he spoke:

"We shall take Athens, and if they must spill blood for a hundred days, so be it, for I will take the city and this world. Every such place I have come across has fallen to me. Every God I have confronted has been destroyed. This world is my greatest challenge, but shall also be my greatest victory."

Jezebel answered her God thus:

"I have faith in you, My Lord, but be cautious. Be mindful of your limitations."

"Your counsel is noted," spoke Baal, "but you said so yourself: these mortals are no match for me, and there are no more Gods left in this world to challenge my rule."

In this, Baal did not know he was wrong, and despite his wounds and weakened powers, it was this brash arrogance that stood as his greatest weakness of all.

As the night went deeper and the moon shined high above, the men of Athens lay the slain body of Dexamenus into a funeral pyre. Amyclas and the others honored him, and his shield was hung up above the gates of Athens to signify his spirit and memory.

Mahria, who lay in her bed, watched Gaia stand on the balcony and look out onto the city. The Earth Mother closed the doors and bid Mahria to sleep, whose thoughts about Theos were restless and anxious. Gaia soothed her worries, and like a mother tending to a frightened child, Gaia held Mahria until she fell asleep.

The night proved uneventful, and the morning came quickly.

So began the Third Day.

At the first signs of the waking sun, when the clouds are a dull gray and the stars wither in their light, Baal marched his army towards the walls of Athens with its ladders and war machines. Amyclas opted to hold the walls rather than charge out, forcing the battle to be one of attrition. The Amazons rained down their arrows, and when the many ladders reached the walls, Amyclas bellowed and hollered to his forces to hold their ground.

As Baal's army began its ascent upon the walls of Athens, many of the ladders were tipped and toppled; sending screaming men down back to the ground below. Yet, the ladders were numerous and spread out, so much so that not all could be reached, and soon, grueling combat began atop the walls. So narrow was the space in which they fought that no more than a handful of men fought at each end where the ladders reached. There were those who simply stood ready, waiting their turn to take the space of a man or Amazon slain in front of them.

The fighting raged for hours, and the walls were piled with the dead and dying. The catapults of Atlantis battered the thick walls of Athens, but the stonework was unmatched, and the catapults could not yet break through. It was then, in the mid afternoon hours, that Baal ordered forward the ram of bronze to breakdown the mighty gate of Athens. Under the watchful eye of Lucifer, no less than sixty men, thirty to a side, pushed the great ram towards the gates of Athens. Amyclas saw their approach, and cried out to the men below in the streets. Quickly, Lamedon and Zarex mustered their soldiers.

There they stood, ready in defense, their shields and spears forming a great wall that even brave men thought twice about charging. Soon, the walls began to rattle with the ram's strikes, and Lamedon, with his mighty shield, braced the gate with all his might. Several others rushed up to aid him, for they knew that if the gates were to fall, the armies of Baal would flood the streets of Athens.

The gate began to splinter and crack, and Iphito, the Amazon, hurried quickly. She and her warriors used torches to set aflame their arrows, and they shot down in an attempt to set the ram ablaze.

Their aim was true, but the ram's bronze plating was too thick. Several of the men operating the great machine were set ablaze, and they rolled like hapless hogs on the ground; the fire eating and crackling at their flesh. Others began to run, only to be pierced by Iphito's unmatched aim.

Lucifer did not take kind to this cowardice, and serving his God, he took hold of the ram and continued to break down the gate. Iphito's arrows glanced off his thick armor, and Lucifer's mighty strength was something of awe and fear to the men who watched from high atop the walls. Lamedon and several others held the gate with their shields, and Zarex stood firm with his men behind, ready for whatever might come were the gates to fall.

Soon, the inhuman power of Lucifer was too great, and the gates of Athens were smashed asunder with the Atlantian ram. Lamedon and those who stood with their shield were thrown back, and Lucifer walked upon them.

Brave,
Thusly did stand Lamedon and Zarex
with their shields and spears held firm in grasp,
The towering frame of Lucifer's might
casting down a shadow upon the men.

Like flies buzzing unto the stale corpse
of a killed bull left to rot in the grass,
So, too, did the men of Atlantis flood
forth from the broken down gates of Athens,
A flowing river of metal and blood.

Amyclas, the Spartan warrior bold,
Leapt from the high walls of Athens above
with his spear striking down on those below,
Savage and fierce in his gaze like a wolf
hungry after a long, cold winter's glaze.

The joint armies held so firmly their ground,
The toll of passage they charged heavily
with their thrusting bronze,
blood be their coinage.

Lamedon,
With his shield and spear clutched in his grasp
looked upon Lucifer, who swung madly
at those all around, blighting them with death.
Fearlessly he charged, throwing his spear true,
The tip finding the chest of Lucifer.

Yet, Lamedon's straight throw was halted quick,
Lucifer's armor held, thick and rigid,
And so the spear tip peeled back and snapped.
Lamedon drew his sword and braced himself
as Lucifer struck down upon him hard.

The hero fell, his shield split in half,
and he scampered to his feet in quick haste.
It was then that brave Zarex leapt forth, too,
His spear striking Lucifer in the side,
The thick armor withholding the sharp point
from piercing through into the fragile ribs.

Leaping,
So did Lucifer with spear and shield
lunge upon brave Zarex with raging might,
The spear tip glancing the hero's chest plate,
Searing into the bronze like a hot stone
dropped into a layer of icy snow.
Zarex was valiant in his fighting,
But his breath waned and muscles ached.

His sword strikes grew tired.
His shield dropped.
He fell.
Death.

Zarex crumpled to the might of Lucifer, and Amyclas let out a cry that blistered the ears of those around. He charged towards Lucifer, cutting down the men who followed Baal with merciless apathy. The joint armies of Athens held firm and did not break at the onslaught, and soon, the armies of Baal grew tired, and the men of Atlantis began to retreat. Lucifer, not taking kindly to this act of cowardice, continued his path of destruction through the ranks of men. It was then that Gaia, watching the battle from the balcony of the royal palace, soared down in the form of a hawk. Mahria cried out for her to not go, but her pleas were unheard.

Gaia, upon reaching the ground, took her true form, and stood before Lucifer in her glowing elegance. She let fly a mighty wind that sent the armies of Baal soaring, with many of the men smashing against the walls of Athens; their souls crushed out of their mortal shells. Lucifer stood firm, but it was then that a crack of lightning struck down, and Lucifer was of no match to the powers of the Earth Mother. He, too, was tossed aside and out beyond the walls of Athens. Gaia, weak from her exertion, collapsed to her knees, and quickly, Amyclas ordered men to help Gaia to her feet. The Amazons continued to rain death down upon those who fled, and Baal, seeing his army flee and regroup behind their lines, cried out in a raging frustration that shook the trees and stirred the sky.

So ended the Third Day.

Gaia was shepherded back to the palace, where she lay down to rest as Mahria tended to her. King Codrus and Amyclas quickly had the men and women of Athens help repair the gates, and the great ram, left behind, was torn apart and used to patch the gateway. Iphito and her Amazon warriors kept watch over the field, out beyond which the camps of Baal's army stood quiet. The body of Zarex was gathered, his death was honored, and his sword was placed above the gates of Athens as testament to his bravery.

The night proved quiet again, and Amyclas had learned that the dead and wounded were many.

So it was that when morning came, the joint armies were mustered into their formation. The Amazons, led by Iphito, looked out over them from atop the high walls. The men below stood with overlapping shields, and their shape was that of a crescent moon with the city to their backs. Down among them stood Amyclas and the others, their armors battered and stained from the two days of war they had thus endured.

So began the Fourth Day.

Baal ordered his army forward, and the men of Atlantis, weary but still hungry with greed, obeyed their God. The catapults from afar bombarded the city with urns of the liquid fire, and a great many lives were lost to their searing touch. The walls were showered again with stones, and the fine masonry was beginning to fail and weaken. Lucifer led the men of Atlantis out onto the field, and when they drew near, they charged upon the joint armies of Athens.

A wave of flesh and metal cascading
across a shore of bright glistening bronze,
Vultures that are hungry for the soon dead
are the gulls that patrol this sea of blood.

Their imminent feast to be a great one!

Eioneus, a whirlwind of swords,
Plowing through the ranks of his enemy
with the ease of a summer's tepid breeze,
His two blades shimmer in the morning light
as they harvest the souls of the wretched.

Yet, for glory, he pays in arrogance,
For Eioneus wandered deep and far
into the mighty ranks of Baal's army.
Like a cub that wanders too far from home,
So can a man be easily preyed on.

Eioneus brave,
With his swinging blades,
Charged Lucifer with courage in his heart,
The flames of a raging vengeance burning
deep in the core of his wild spirit.
How the hero spun
and weaved through the swarm
of flesh and metal that surrounded him.

The sword held firm in his left hand shattered
upon striking Lucifer's thick armor,
The sword held firm in his right hand hit true,
Cracking the bronze plate of Lucifer's chest.

So he struck down again, now hacking flesh,
And the dark warrior bellowed in pain,
Tasting the agonizing, sharp feel
of bronze searing into his tender flesh.

Leaping,
So did Lucifer with spear and shield
fall upon Eioneus with his strength,
The spear tip glancing the hero's armor,
Cutting into the bronze like the sharp tooth
of a Lion stabbing into his prey.
Eioneus was brave in his fighting,
But his breath waned and muscles ached.
His sword strikes grew tired.
His knees buckled.
He fell.
Death.

Eioneus' agility was no more. His lifeless body fell limp to the ground, but Lucifer, now wounded, let out a cry that deafened those around. The joint armies of Athens held firm their lines, and soon, Baal's army retreated yet again back towards their camps. The catapults were withdrawn with haste, and Lucifer himself, enraged, scampered with the rest of the men, of whom many were pierced through by the Amazon's arrows.

Baal, seeing all this unfold, stared upon Athens with exasperated eyes. How could it be that this final bastion of hope for a people, Godless and besieged, could hold their ground for so long? Baal cared not for the answer, for as quickly as the thought did drift through his mind, he again felt assured of his victory. Athens could not hold out much longer, and with the wounded and dead mounting, their fate will come in due time.

Amyclas and the others were quick to shepherd the wounded, and they collected and carried back to the city the body of Eioneus. His broken sword, the one that had wounded Lucifer and proved him mortal, was placed on the wall of Athens so that his deed would inspire. The sun set, the sentries of the two armies stared at eachother across the dark void, and night came with no signs of victory or defeat for either.

So ended the Fourth Day.

During the night, King Codrus held a council with his advisors and the four remaining commanders. It was soon revealed that their food stores were dwindling, there was a great number of wounded, and illness was starting to spread amongst the people forced to reside densely in squalor. When it was asked for how much longer the city could hold, the advisors lamented that it could be no more than two days. Yet, this number was also estimated to be but only one day, for the catapults of Atlantis had done great damage to the walls and gate. King Codrus and the others then knew that if Theos, the young God and son of Zeus, did not return in time, the city would surely fall to Baal.

Amyclas was also faced with the dire news that his army's numbers were ravaged. To avoid any more open fighting on the field where this could be taken advantage of by Baal, it was decided that they would hold the walls and gate. Their plan of defeating the army of Atlantis was no longer achievable. They were now to survive through the grueling trial of attrition, and hope for their God's return.

The commanders went to rest their weary minds and spirits. The sentries stared into the void, but the night proved quiet.

So began the Fifth Day.

When the sun's light peaked over the mountain tops, dulling the glow of the stars and bathing the fields in a lavender hue, Baal ordered the men of Atlantis to repair what ladders they still had. Amyclas and King Codrus watched from high atop the walls of Athens.

"Let them come to us," said the King. "Let them die on our walls."

As Baal's army marched towards the city, Amyclas ordered the battle lines to their formations. He, Iphito, and Hyperbius would hold the walls with their warriors, while Lamedon and King Codrus would secure the streets of Athens with their battalions were the gates to fall. Baal, who was wise to the ways of war, knew that when the fields stood empty, his enemies were daring him to take the walls.

So it was that the men of Atlantis marched with their ladders and war machines under the shadows of Amazonian arrows. The catapults continued their barrage, battering the worn out walls and raining fire. Ladders reached the ramparts once again, and the soldiers of Atlantis flooded the walls and clashed with Greek and Amazon alike.

The fighting raged on, and Baal, keen on joining, stared off into the city with Jezebel at his side. Gaia stood on the balcony of the palace, staring over the bloodied walls and field into the eyes of the false God.

"She is weaker," spoke Baal. "Soon, I shall be able to defeat her and end this."

"But killing the Spirit Mother will destroy this world," answered Jezebel. "Do you not wish to rule over it?"

Baal waited, thinking for a moment. The false God then spoke:

"No. This world is not worth the troubles of ruling. Let it be destroyed, so that I may conquer another, more deserving, world."

"Why waste your power then? Why not leave this place, so that you may heal?" asked Jezebel of her God.

"No," he answered. "I will not let them taste even the faintest of victory. Watch how they blindly kill eachother, not knowing that in the end, they, too, shall lay rotting into the soil."

And so, the fighting raged, and the men of Atlantis were driven by false promises of wealth and fame. The fighting on the walls was fierce and plodding, and there were many bodies to be burned and honored that night. The catapults continued their terror, and the stonework of the Athenian walls began to falter. Hyperbius of Thebes would not allow the walls to be penetrated, so he mustered thirty of his bravest men and sought out Amyclas. Hyperbius gave unto him his shield and spoke:

"Spartan! Take my shield and hang it over the gate with the swords and shields of the others," said he, "for I have seen the last of life."

Amyclas could not question these words, for Hyperbius and his thirty men stormed out of the city with haste. The hero, with spear and torch in hand, raced across the field, cutting down all in his way with a grace in his strides.

Like a leopard that which hunts in tall grass,
Running with an elegance, fierce and strong,
So, too, was Hyperbius in his hunt
across the bloodied fields of Athens.

Hyperbius and his men reached the war machines, and their Atlantian crews fought bitterly to protect them. The enemy was outmatched, and the catapults were set aflame. The urns of liquid fire burned and smoldered. Lucifer was quick to notice, and he led men to cut off Hyperbius' escape. The brave warrior had nowhere to go, and so it was that he stood firm to meet his fate.

Brave Hyperbius! Stand firm, like a rock!

Leaping,
So did Lucifer with sword and shield
fall upon Hyperbius with his strength,
The sword edge cutting the hero's armor,
Thrust into the bronze like a woodsman's axe
felling a mighty tree in the forest.
Hyperbius was brave in his fighting,
But his breath waned and muscles ached.
His sword strikes grew tired.
His knees buckled.
He fell.
Death.

Lucifer cut down Hyperbius, and all thirty men whom had risked their lives for eternal honor perished from Atlantian bronze. The catapults, however, were destroyed, and this angered Baal greatly. He again reached for his scabbard, wanting to pull out the flaming sword and charge into the fight, but Jezebel stopped him.

"No, my Lord," she spoke. "Until the walls are taken, you cannot risk wasting what energy you have."

Baal listened, and despite his urge to disregard this counsel, the dark God heeded it, and did not join the fight. The men of Atlantis again fell back from the hard defended walls, carrying what ladders they could. Their wounded and dead were just as great as those of Athens, and Baal stared out towards the balcony far in the distance where Gaia stood, watching.

Night came. The stars emerged.

So ended the Fifth Day.

Amyclas, Lamedon, Iphito, and King Codrus held council. The food stores were barren, the sick and wounded were many, and the streets of the city were overflowing with filth. The empty granaries were quickly packed with women and children, and every building that stood, even the temples, were filled with people so that the streets would be empty of the innocent. The joint army of Athens rested, knowing that their time of great victory, or utter destruction, was drawing near.

The sun rose, and so began the Sixth Day.

The morning dew had only just settled when the armies of Atlantis again charged and mounted the walls with their ladders. The exhausted men fought in their battle lines, losing and gaining momentum on the narrow walls in alternation. Baal watched with a growing fury, wanting to test his Godly strength, but the cold stare of Gaia dissuaded him with every glance. Could it be that he *feared* her? The memory of her immense power was still fresh in the dark God's thoughts, but she, too, was weaker now.

"When the walls are ours," Jezebel would whisper, "we will strike down in force."

Late into the afternoon hours, the clouds began to gather, and snow began to fall. Men slipped and tumbled on the bloodied walls, and soon, the fortunes of war shifted to that of the Atlantians. Lucifer, with his hulking strength and imposing figure, had climbed up a ladder close to the main gatehouse, and slaughtered any man who challenged him.

Brave Lamedon, with his mighty shield, defended the gatehouse with his life. A many number of Atlantians drew their final breath at the behest of his spear, and it was not long before Lucifer and he clashed with their bronze.

Like the mother bear defending her cubs,
Guarding the mouth of her cave with her life,
Jaws snapping at the hungry, vicious wolves
that encircle her.

So did Lamedon fight with bold honor
to keep the gatehouse from enemy hands,
A mountain standing
firm in the harsh winds.

Leaping,
So did Lucifer with spear and shield
fall upon brave Lamedon with his strength,
The spear tip piercing the hero's armor,
Thrust in like a fisherman's javelin
that which ensnares the day's bountiful catch.
Lamedon was fearless in his fighting,
But his breath waned and muscles ached.

His spear strikes grew tired.
His knees buckled.
He fell.
Death.

Lamedon was slain, and his limp body rolled over the wall and into the blood sodden dirt below. The Atlantians stormed the gatehouse, and Amyclas cried out for the men to hold firm in the streets. Iphito and her Amazons abandoned the walls quickly to join the defense below. The Atlantians opened the mighty gate of Athens, and they stormed into the city. Baal, watching from afar, grew bold, and he stared out at Gaia who still stood on the balcony.

Their eyes met, and they sensed the impending end.

Amyclas and his men held firm in the streets, as not one route into the inner city was not blockaded with the shields and spears of King Codrus' warriors. Lucifer leapt down from the wall and ravaged their ranks, and it was then that Amyclas and Iphito attacked the mighty warrior.

Fury,
Raging fury,
With the fires of war burning his soul,
The Spartan warrior charged with a roar,
His spear point seething into Lucifer
and piercing straight through
his battered armor.

Haste,
Quick haste,
Iphito of the Amazons let her
swift arrows fly forth
deadly straight and true,
Harassing Lucifer like stinging bees
do the greedy bear.

Leaping,
So did Lucifer with spear and shield
fall upon brave Amyclas with his strength,
But the Spartan commander was fearless
in spirit and heart,
Fighting with all his mortal strength and skill.
But his breath waned and muscles ached.
His spear strikes grew tired.
His knees buckled.
He fell,
But Death shall wait!

Dying,
In final breath and gasp, Amyclas struck
with all his power,
His wounds great and deep.
The Spartan's spear sank into Lucifer,
Like a hunter's knife into the deft deer,
Striking his dark and wretched, beating heart.

Life, slipping from eyes,
The soul, spirited into the far skies,
Death unto them both.

Lucifer was struck down by Amyclas, who felt the warmth of life slowly leave his body. His men all cried out, rallied by the death of Lucifer and the sacrifice of their leader, and pushed back against the Atlantians. Baal, seeing that his mighty warrior had been slain, let out a cry of anguish that shook the ground. He could wait no longer, and pulled forth the flaming sword. In great pain and forfeit of his already fractured powers, Baal unfurled the wings of a black hawk from the flesh of his back, and he soared into the city of Athens with his wrath. Jezebel ran promptly towards the main gate, in awe of her God, and thirsty for the taste of mortal blood.

Jezebel leapt upon men with her sharp teeth, gashing open their necks with deep bites of voracious satisfaction. Iphito saw her, and let loose her arrows to kill this vile creature. Jezebel was agile, and she pounced upon Iphito with her jagged teeth and nails that jutted forth like claws. She slashed the Amazon across her face, but the warrior was skilled, and she pulled from her scabbard of bronze and leathers a short, curved blade with which she cut off Jezebel's left hand.

The depraved fiend wailed and shrieked in agony, and Iphito ended her suffering with a swift slash to the neck. The Amazon looked to see Baal come crashing down from the sky with his flaming sword, hacking through the men of Athens and inciting upon them a fear and dread that gave the Atlantians newfound spirit. So ferocious was the sight of Baal that men who were once brave now fled like cowering children.

It was then that Gaia, from the balcony of the palace, looked to Mahria and bid her to have faith. She then, in the form of an eagle, swooped down into the city and landed in a brilliant flash of light before Baal.

Light,
Robes flowing in the breeze's soft whisper,
A sword of white bronze shimmering in light
clutched in her soft hand.

Eyes,
Piercing green, staring into the dark God,
Igniting memories of their past clash,
Beckoning him to challenge her again.

Rage,
Bounding forth with insatiable rage,
So did Baal with his daunting sword of flames
fall upon Gaia in the lust of war,
The beat of bronze upon bronze all around
the music that incites a man's spirit.

Watch in awe, you men and women of Greece!
Watch the dark God, seized by the madness of
wretched avarice,
Eyes ablaze with the fires of conquest!

Watch in awe, you men and women of Greece!
Watch the Earth Mother, like a silken scarf
ensnared in the winds of a mighty storm,
Fight with a grace and beauty thus unmatched.

Gaia and Baal battled fiercely, and the Earth Mother, with her power waning from exhaustion, split the ground with a thunderous cry that devoured Baal and much of the Atlantian army. Empty buildings and the battered gatehouse of Athens slipped into the dark abyss. The Amazons and what remained of the joint Athenian army watched in awe and wonder the great destruction that lay sprawled before them. What remained of the Atlantian army dispersed, and they ran like ants scurrying from rain off into the surrounding fields. Gaia, weak and beaten, collapsed to the ground with heavy breaths.

It was then that Baal, with his beating wings, soared out of the abyss with his flaming sword, and he pounced towards the frail Earth Mother. He swung his sword down, seething through the air with his fury, but the dark God did not account for the bravery of heroic men. King Codrus threw himself with selfless valor before Baal, and with his shield, stopped the strike of the flaming sword from hitting Gaia. Instead, the sword smoldered through the warrior King's shield and mortally wounded him, to which there were many gasps and cries of anguish. Codrus, with his last breath, jabbed his spear, but Baal grabbed and flung him aside, dashing the brave King into a mound of rubble.

Baal turned his attention again to Gaia, but it was then that, like lightning from the sky, the Spear of Achilles came roaring down from the Heavens and crashed into the soil before him. The force of the strike sent a wave of dust and wind that threw Baal back from the Earth Mother, and it was then that the men and women of Athens laid their eyes upon Theos.

So returned the Last God!

Theos landed with Pegasus and retrieved His spear, the very sight of Him warming the aching and tired hearts of every man, woman, and child there. Baal, in his anguish, took to the skies and soared towards the peak of Olympus. The Amazons fired their arrows after him, but they were useless against his Godly might. Theos looked to the balcony of the palace, where He saw the gleaming eyes and glowing smile of Mahria, and then turned to Iphito and spoke:

"Tend to Gaia, and have your warriors shepherd the dead and dying."

And so, Theos took flight with Pegasus to pursue Baal. Through the falling snow and graying skies, the young God chased the dark one to the peak of Olympus, where the two finally landed amidst the ruins of the once mighty Pantheon.

-VII-ASCENSION OF THE CROSS-VII-

~The last enemy to be destroyed is death~
1 Corinthians 15:26

Snow, Gently falling,
Blanketing this ancient ground,
Frozen tears of mourning for a time
long dead and gone.

Hallow soil where the Gods did once die,
Hallow soil where a new God is crowned.

Theos, with the armor and weapons of the ancient heroes, landed with Pegasus, and bid her to fly off into the sky for safety. The winged horse took to the clouds as the young God readied His spear and shield. He looked to Baal, who stared upon Him with a maddened glare.

"Are you *it* that gives this wretched world its hope?" asked Baal.

To this, Theos responded:

"The name my mortal father gave me is Kristos. The name my father in Heaven gave me is Theos. To honor them both, my name is Theos Kristos. I am the son of Zeus, and the last true

God of Man and its realms. I have come to claim my throne as King of Earth and its Heavens. Hear me, Baal, for my judgment has come for you! I am *God*!"

Silence across the windswept ruins.

Baal stared upon this young deity with burning eyes. The flaming sword sat in its sheath, and the dark God had no intention of using it yet. Baal held out his hand, and in that instant, the clouds above did split. There came crashing down, like thunder, the spear of blackened bronze into Baal's hands with which he had slain the Titans and Olympians long before.

Baal now remembered this child.

"If you proclaim yourself God of this world," so spoke Baal, "then you, too, shall die as those who came before you."

And so it was that Baal, with his Godly might, flung his spear at Theos. Its tip dug deep into the Shield of Ajax, and the young Theos was thrown back at the power of this strike, but the legendary shield held firm and Theos stood unscathed. The young God ripped the black spear out of His shield, and shattered it against the ruined marble pillars.

Baal, not taking heed of his weakened state, drew his flaming sword and leapt upon Theos with every remnant of his strength and anger.

Thus the ascension of the Cross!
So began the fall of Baal,
So began the rise of the Lord.

Charging,
With a cry that split the winds around,
Baal let roar his voice in angst and hatred,
Swinging wildly with his flaming blade,
God battling God,
Windswept snow dancing around their fury.

Splitting,
So was the Shield of Ajax then split,
Cut in half by the sword sweltering hot,
Like paper ignited by a lone spark.
So was the spear of Achilles then dropped
into the cold snow.

Swinging,
Theos pulled forth the Sword of Peleus,
Stabbing and slicing at Baal with its edge,
Parrying and avoiding the hot blows
of the scorching blade,
Fire eating the ice where it then touched,

Melting marble and rock with every missed
swing hacked and taken.

Shattered,
How Baal, with his grip, grabbed the razor edge
of the Sword of Peleus, gleaming bronze,
and crushed it within his hand with brute force,
Shards splintering, tears of metal falling
to the frozen ground.

Seething,
So did the sword of Baal burn and incise
a mark across the chest of Theos brave,
The holy Aegis guarding His soft flesh
with heavy bronze plate.
A blow found its mark upon His plumed helm,
And Theos staggered,
The helmet swiped off His head and fractured.

Lunging,
So did Baal fall upon Theos in rage,
Swinging down his blade,
The young God upon His back in the snow.

Grabbing,
So did Theos reach and take hold firmly
the Spear of Achilles from the cold ice,

But the sword of Baal did sever it half,
And the dark God swung down again in wrath.

The Cross of God!
Theos took hold of the two spear segments,
Crossing them before his face for defense,
The flaming sword of Baal sweltering hot
then did smash unto
the two bronze pieces.
So intense were the flames and searing heat
that the two halves of the heroic spear
melded into one,
Taking the form of the Holy Lord's Cross!

With a mighty effort, Theos knocked Baal back and off His frame, so that He may rise with the Cross in hand. Baal charged wildly with his strength and sanity waning, but the young God of Man was ready. With the sharp point of the spear still intact and forming the left arm of the Cross, Theos cried out in rage and swung, plunging the spear tip into Baal's ribs. His armor chipped and the tip found flesh, causing the false one to scream and moan in agony. Theos then ripped the point out from Baal's flesh, and with a mighty swing of the Cross, thrust the sharp tip into the side of Baal's head.

Life,
Fleeting,
Flowing away like a roaring river
fattened by a thawing, northern winter coat.

Tumble,
Lifeless,
Falling to the ground with limp, flailing limbs,
An empty shell with no rightful purpose.
Death.

So did Baal, with the glistening of his eyes burned out, fall into the snow. Exhausted, Theos looked upon the body of the dark God, which turned to cinders and ash blown off into the air with a gust of wind. The song of the whispering breeze across the desolate remnants of the once mighty Pantheon was one of a quiet victory. Theos whistled, and Pegasus came down from the sky. He took to her back, and the young God made His way back down to Athens.

In the city, man, woman, and child helped gather the dead and wounded. Iphito and Mahria tended to Gaia in the royal chambers, and it was then that Theos descended from the sky. Many were in awe of His presence, and many more did cheer and celebrate His triumphant return. Theos took to the palace and was led to where Gaia lay, resting. Mahria bid Him a long and loving welcome, one filled with kisses and warm embraces, after which Theos took to Gaia's side and proclaimed:

"It is done."

Gaia nodded, assuring the young God that she would regain her strength and aid Him in His rule, for He was now one God tasked with the work of many. So it is why evil and calamity still exists under His watchful eye.

Iphito, the Amazon and lone survivor of the seven commanders, bowed and paid respect to the new God. Theos bid her rise, and honored her for her bravery and resoluteness. He gave to her the Cross, forged in battle with the two fragments of the Spear of Achilles, and spoke thusly:

"Iphito, you brave woman and warrior who held her Faith as firm as she did her spear, sword, shield, and bow. Take this and journey to the four corners of the known world. Brandish it as a symbol of my victory-our victory-and let the world know that it has a new

God; one that will protect and serve His people with every facet of His power. Let this be a symbol of your Faith, and the Faith of those who acknowledge me. Go. Be my messenger, my *Apostolos*, and serve as my champion."

So it was then that Iphito took the Cross that struck down Baal, and embarked on her journey to spread the news and words of the new Lord. When night came, the people of Athens lamented and honored King Codrus for his act of selflessness, and there was great celebration of life, death, and victory.

So ended the Sixth Day.

When morning came, the city of Athens rested in peace, and Gaia herself recuperated from her exertions and trials. Theos spent time with His beloved Mahria, and so it was that the Seventh Day was to be celebrated as a day of rest, and the seven day week was created.

Mahria tearfully told Him that she carried His child, and to this, Theos was elated. The young God, however, had one more task at hand, and so the next day, He bid Mahria farewell, but gave promise of a quick return. Theos left

Athens on the back of Pegasus, and soared off and away towards the city of Atlantis.

When the Lord of Man arrived at the city, King Ahabikos rushed forth from his palace. God had landed on the outskirts of the city, and bemoaned that Ahabikos had betrayed his own world by aiding Baal with his armies and war machines. Ahabikos recanted his actions, but God, who was known to be merciful, did not take to heart the vile King's words. So, Theos summoned Gaia, and the Earth Mother split the ground and made the ocean swell and sway.

The city of Atlantis was sunk into the depths of the world, with its entire people paying with their lives for greed, deception, and indolence.

Theos returned to Athens, where He came back to Mahria as promised, and took her to Olympus. There, Gaia gave unto Mahria the immortality of a Goddess, so that she and Theos may rebuild the Pantheon. The Earth Mother, however, warned the young God that His trials had only begun, and that the universe hid evils far darker than that of Baal. Theos, overlooking His Kingdom of Earth from high atop Olympus, looked to Mahria and touched her belly, knowing well His child slept soundly within.

"If such dangers are to yet come," spoke He, "then I shall be ready."

And so Theos, the slayer of Baal, the God of Man whose symbol was that of the Cross, began His rule of the Earth as Lord, Protector, and Judge.

-Ω-EPILOGOS-Ω-

Children,
Sleep, little ones,
Dream of this mythic tale,
Extolled and marked with sacrifice
so that our world may still live.

May the bards sing of Them,
May the poets write of Them,
May history be kind to Them,
May we remember Them.

Children,
Sleep, little ones,
Dream of this mythic tale,
Dream of the land where Heroes great did tread,
May His Grace bless you little one,
Amen.

www.ingramcontent.com/pod-product-compliance
Lightning Source LLC
LaVergne TN
LVHW091001080826
845145LV00003B/1085

* 9 7 8 0 6 1 5 8 8 5 9 8 8 *